# *Blame It On His Gangsta Luv 2*

## *Tina J*

## *2018*

@ Facebook Author T M Jenkins

*This novel is a work of fiction. Any resemblances to actual events, real people, living or dead, organizations, establishments or locales are products of the author's imagination. Other names, characters, places, and incidents are used fictionally.*



*Because of the dynamic nature of the Internet, any web address or links contained in this book may have changed since publication and may no longer be valid.*

## *More books from me:*

**The Thug I Chose 1, 2 & 3**

**A Thin Line Between Me and My Thug 1 & 2**

**I Got Luv For My Shawty 1 & 2**

**Kharis and Caleb: A Different Kind of Love 1 & 2**

**Loving You Is A Battle 1 & 2 & 3**

**Violet and The Connect 1 & 2 & 3**

**You Complete Me**

**Love Will Lead You Back**

**This Thing Called Love**

**Are We In This Together 1,2 &3**

**Shawty Down To Ride For a Boss 1, 2 &3**

**When A Boss Falls in Love 1, 2 & 3**

**Let Me Be The One 1 & 2**

**We Got That Forever Love**

**Aint No Savage Like The One I Got 1&2**

**A Queen and A Hustla 1, 2 & 3**

**Thirsty For A Bad Boy 1&2**

**Hassan and Serena: An Unforgettable Love 1&2**

**Caught Up Loving A Beast 1, 2 & 3**

**A Street King And His Shawty 1 & 2**

**I Fell For The Wrong Bad Boy 1&2**

**I Wanna Love You 1 & 2**

**Addicted to Loving a Boss 1, 2, & 3**

**I Need That Gangsta Love 1&2**

**Creepin With The Plug 1 & 2**

**All Eyes On The Crown 1,2&3**

**When She's Bad, I'm Badder: Jiao and Dreek, A Crazy Love Story 1,2&3**

**Still Luvin A Beast 1&2**

**Her Man, His Savage 1 & 2**

**Marco & Rakia: Not Your Ordinary, Hood Kinda Love 1,2 & 3**

**Feenin For A Real One 1, 2 & 3**

**A Kingpin's Dynasty 1, 2 & 3**

**What Kinda Love Is This: Captivating A Boss 1, 2 & 3**

**Frankie & Lexi: Luvin A Young Beast 1, 2 & 3**

**A Dope Boys Seduction 1, 2 & 3**

**My Brother's Keeper 1. 2 & 3**

**C'Yani & Meek: A Dangerous Hood Love 1, 2 & 3**

**When A Savage Falls for A Good Girl 1, 2 & 3**

**Eva & Deray 1 & 2**

**Blame It On His Gangsta Luv**

# Synopsis

# Blame It On His Gangsta Luv 2

Yariah and Caleek finally took the step at being a couple. They made future plans and were now expecting their own bundle of joy. Nothing or no one could ruin their happiness except Tasheem who popped up outta nowhere.

Caleek is stuck between his past and future because he doesn't know who to believe. Can he forgive Yariah if it comes out she's the one who abducted his ex or will he dig deeper and find the truth to clear her name?

Tasheem returned from the dead, however; she was alive and well. Of course she accused Yariah as being the woman who committed the acts on her but is she right? Did the woman she despised years ago conspire to have her killed? In Tasheem's mind, her accusation is correct until they go to court and something makes her doubt everything she thought she knew.

Cazi took a DNA test for Destiny, yet the results are not what he expected. With Amara stuck in the hospital, time is of the essence for him to reveal the truth. He doesn't want to cause her any pain but he finds out some disturbing things his wife has done in the past and will have to find a way to handle it. He now has to step up and do what's right but what happens when he tries and it's too late?

Table of Contents

# ***Warning:***

This book is strictly Urban Fiction and the story is

# **NOT REAL**!

Characters will not behave the way you want them to; nor will they react to situations the way you think they should. Some of them may be drug addicts, kingpins, savages, thugs, rich, poor, ho's, sluts, haters, bitter ex-girlfriends or boyfriends, people from the past and the list can go on and on. That is what Urban Fiction mostly consists of. If this isn't anything you foresee yourself interested in, then do yourself a favor and don't read it because it's only going to piss you off. □□

Also, the book will not end the way you want so please be advised that the outcome will be based solely on my own thoughts and ideas. I hope you enjoy this book. Thanks so much to my readers, supporters, publisher and fellow authors and authoress for the support. □□

***Previously…***

# *Lori*

I paced back and forth outside the reception after Caleek embarrassed fuck outta me. I wasn't blind to the fact he loved the Yariah bitch but why was he tryna make her his woman when we're expecting? Did he really think I'd be ok with her fucking up our relationship? He had another thing coming if he thought I'd take this shit lying down.

Then I come out and see them fucking in the same truck we've been in numerous times. I knew they were doing something because it was rocking. I wonder if she'd be mad knowing I sucked him off in here the day he supposedly broke up with me. Don't he know there is no breaking up with us?

I rolled my eyes when he walked past me smirking. I don't know why he thought shit was funny because I planned on making his life a living hell now. Once this child comes, he's gonna either be with me or wish he never fucked up and came inside my womb. It's gonna really suck to be him and if this bitch planned on being with him, she's gonna see a lot of me too.

"Get out the truck." I shouted after knocking on the window. Most people roll the window down and let you talk but this bitch really got out. I had to step back to give us a little space. I'm not fighter but ain't no bitch gonna hit me either.

"What?"

"Why couldn't you leave my man alone?" She laughed.

"I left your man alone but as you can see, it's meant to be between us." Now it was my turn to laugh.

"You say it's meant to be, but it wouldn't have been had his previous girl not died." Her face turned up. I could tell that shit hit a nerve and kept going.

"Yea you thought it was all about you over the years but he ain't even think about proposing to you." I smirked.

"You would've been the same side bitch you've been since he and I were together."

"Side bitch? I had a man."

"Yup a man who cheated on you."

"Who the fuck told you that?"

"It doesn't really matter now does it? What matters is you thinking what he did to me is ok and that when the next bitch comes around, he won't do you the same?"

"One thing I'm not worried about is him doing me the same." She moved closer to me.

"See what you fail to realize is you and his ex Tasheem were just substitutes until the woman he wanted was ready. Everyone knows where his heart is and whether you admit it or not, you know it's the truth."

"Tha fuck you doing Lori?" I heard Caleek yelling as he walked towards us.

"Listening to her say Tasheem meant nothing to you and she's the one you wanted to marry." I knew Tasheem was a soft spot for him.

"She ain't lying so what?" My mouth dropped and the bitch smirked.

"Don't say shit else to my woman and if I find out you did, I'm gonna make sure you regret it. Get in sexy." He opened the door and waited for her to get situated. He turned to me, looked me up and down and shook his head.

"I thought you were better than this."

"Better than what? Caleek why are you doing this?"

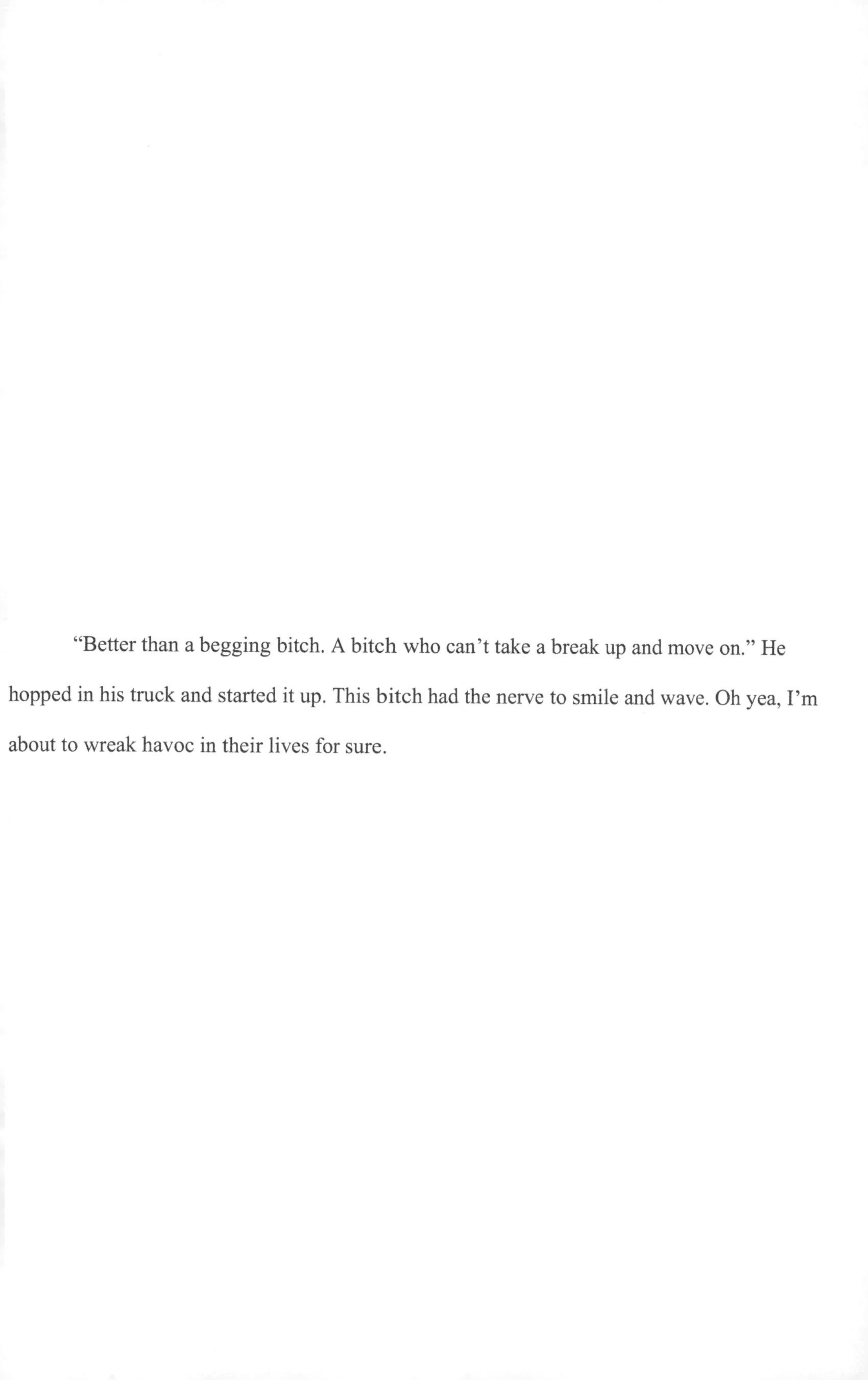

"Better than a begging bitch. A bitch who can't take a break up and move on." He hopped in his truck and started it up. This bitch had the nerve to smile and wave. Oh yea, I'm about to wreak havoc in their lives for sure.

# *Yariah*

"Yariah for as long as I've known you, I can tell when you're hiding something." Amara said as we drove to her and my brother's house. She picked me up from class today because she wanted to talk to me about something important. It sounded serious and I could use the time away from my house. Not that anyone was bothering me, but it felt good to be elsewhere.

"What is it you think I'm hiding?"

"Ever since you and Caleek took it there almost what; three or four months ago you've changed."

"Meaning?"

"You've put on at least five pounds, you no longer dress in fitted clothes and besides going to school you spend more time in the house than out of it. Do you really want me to say it?" She parked in front of the house.

"I'm not ready." I broke down crying again. It seems like it's all I do these days. I wake up, go in the bathroom and cry. I cry if my food don't come out right at the fast food place. I cry at every damn thing.

"Who else knows?"

"No one Amara and I wanna keep it that way. Let me tell when I'm ready."

"OH MY GOD! I'M GONNA BE AN AUNTIE!" She screamed and reached over to hug me. I loved Amara like my own sister. I didn't have any friends and she's the only one I talked to about everything; including Dallas. She also told me to strap up every time we had sex because if a woman can say she's sleeping with your man, true or not, then he's out there doing something he had no business.

I may have gone down on him, but I definitely made him wear condoms and I'm glad I did. He was mad until I explained we weren't ready for kids. He agreed, and we had a lotta protection but come to find out it must've been for me and those other women. To this day he still calls and sends me messages about how sorry he is.

"Cazi is going to be excited and your dad; girl he can't wait for a grand baby." Just as she said that I heard sadness in her voice.

Amara is the love of my brother's life and all he wants is her, kids and to be married. Unfortunately, they're having issues in the pregnancy department and no one can figure out why. The doctors claim both of their bodies are fine, yet no matter how much sex they have no child has been produced. If you ask me, I think if they both stop stressing over it, it'll happen. It's what everyone says anyway.

The two of us stepped out the car and I walked to the back to help with the groceries when outta nowhere a SUV almost ran into the back of the truck. We checked each other out and gave them our fingers. Not sure if they saw us but who cares. Why the fuck were they even that close?

I walked to the driver's side to grab her purse after bringing the bags in, and the same black truck came flying towards us or should I say me. I felt my body being pushed because Amara tossed me in the grass. Sadly, the truck hit her, and I watched as her body flew on top of another car. My body was frozen, and my voice disappeared. I had to have gone into shock because I can't even tell you what happened next.

**********************

"Are you ok?" My father stood over me. I heard monitors beeping and my hands quickly went to my stomach.

"Does he know?" He smiled.

"No and please don't tell him."

"He's with Cazi. He'll be here when they find out about Amara."

"Oh ok."

"Yariah, he came in when you first got here but no one knew you were pregnant. When they did the blood work, he had already gone down the hall to sit with Cazi. You have to tell him." I let a few tears fall down my face.

"I will but I'm scared he'll keep doing the back and forth with us." He rubbed my hair back. I would never admit to the bitch Lori he may do the same thing to me, but I had those feelings for sure.

"I doubt it and you have to take responsibility for your part in it too."

"How?"

"By continuing to sleep with him before he was completely done with her." The nurse came in and I asked her to remove the monitors on my stomach. She declined so I did it myself. I don't want Caleek knowing anything about this child right now.

"I need to check on Amara." My dad helped me out the bed and Aphrodite came in with clothes in her hand.

"How long have I been here?"

"Three hours."

"Three hours? How's my brother? Is he ok? Did they find who did it?"

"No and he's been back and forth to check on you. Amara is in surgery."

"She got hurt bad sis." Aphrodite walked with me in the bathroom.

“How did everyone find out?” I started putting the clothes on and brushed my hair in a ponytail.

“Cazi said he was calling Amara and when she didn’t answer he pulled up the cameras at their house. He saw cops and ambulances there and raced over. One of the neighbors called the cops and gave a description of the truck.”

“Is she ok?”

“We don’t know sis. Cazi said by the time he got there you were in one ambulance and she was in the other. They raced both of y’all in and he’s been downstairs waiting to hear from the doctor.”

“Ok. Let me hurry up because I need to tell them what I remember.” I hurried to finish, signed myself out and walked slow to the room they were in. The doctor advised me to stay but I had to be there for Amara and Cazi.

“Did the doctor come out yet?” I ran, or should I say moved slowly to him.

“What the hell are you doing out the room?” He looked at my dad and sister. Both of them shook their head. They knew I wasn’t gonna sit in bed.

“Cazi, I had to come down. The person was aiming for me.”

“WHAT?”

“I was getting her purse from the truck and she must’ve been in the doorway because I didn’t even know she saw it happen. All I know is the truck aimed for me, she pushed me out the way and…” I stopped and started crying.

“That should’ve been me.” He hugged me tight and told me not to blame myself but how could I not? Whoever it was wanted me for some reason.

"Why aren't you upstairs in the bed." Caleek took me from Cazi and held me. His embrace felt good and all I wanted was to go home and lay up with him.

"I couldn't stay up there knowing she's down here because of me."

"Don't blame yourself Riah." He lifted my face and placed a kiss on my lips.

"When this is over, I'm taking you home. If you're not staying here, then you should be home lying down.

"I agree." I wiped my face.

"I don't wanna keep fighting but she can't keep coming around. If you still want her then leave me alone."

"What are you talking about? You know I don't want her."

"I don't care if it sounds like an ultimatum Caleek. It's me or her."

"It's you Yariah. It's always been you."

"Then you need to make her understand." I pointed to Lori who appeared upset but who knows when she so sneaky. I've watched her put on sad faces in front of him and change up when he turned his back. Something ain't right with her.

# *Caleek*

"Ummm why are you so close to her and what is she talking about her or me? What the fuck am I missing?" Lori was swinging her neck like I won't knock it off her fucking shoulders. I don't for the life of me understand why she continues to ignore me saying Yariah is where I wanna be. She knows we're together and asking why am I close. She gotta be fucking crazy.

"First off, how the fuck did you find me?" I folded my arms and stared at her.

"There's no tracking device on my phone and I haven't spoken to you since we last spoke at the reception."

"You do know Aphrodite is my best friend right?" I glanced over at Ro, who was sitting with Bongi had the same confused look on her face as me.

"Let's talk." I snatched her hand and walked out the door. Everyone didn't need to hear our conversation. When we got by my car, I saw a dark truck with headlights on facing me. I felt for my gun to make sure I could shoot if needed.

"Look, this is my last time telling you we're not gonna work."

"What are you talking about Caleek? We were doing fine before the wedding. Its like whenever you get around Yariah, we break up. What is it about her?"

I smiled listening to her ask about Riah. I can't even tell you how we fell for one another when we've known each other forever. One day she was a snot nose little girl getting on me and Cazi nerves. The next, she was my other best friend and the woman I wanted in my life forever. She's even given me advice on me and Tasheem's relationship knowing how our feelings were for each other. She is definitely the woman I wanna be with.

"She's the woman I'm supposed to be with."

"What about Tasheem?" I snatched her up by the shirt.

"Don't ever discuss Tasheem. You didn't know her." I pushed her away and started walking back towards the hospital.

The car I noticed now turned the lights off and a door opened. I stopped, and the person stepped out. I couldn't tell who it was, and they posed no threat so I continued going in.

"CALEEK! STOP THIS SHIT WITH HER!" I swung the door opened and left her standing there. I saw Riah coming out the bathroom and the doctor walking over to Cazi at the same time.

"Come on." I took her hand in mine and stood behind her as the doctor spoke.

"Hi. I'm Dr. Sampson." He shook hands with everyone here.

"You need to pick up clothes when we leave?" I whispered in Yariah's ear.

"Yea and I'm not staying if she gonna be stalking you." I swung her around to look at me.

"Ain't no stalking and fuck her. It's you and me forever now. I'm about to get you pregnant, we buying a house and getting married."

"It's about time but can you two be quiet so we can hear?" Her pops said, and we laughed. I guess we weren't whispering quietly.

"Mrs. Perry suffered a lot in the accident." I smirked when the doctor called her name because they really jumped the broom and lucky they did because the doctor wouldn't be able to tell him shit if they weren't married.

Her parents were in Jamaica and on their way back so we would've had to wait even longer. I can't imagine how bad he would've flipped if he had to wait.

"She has a broken leg, nose and her pelvis was fractured. Due to the massive amount of scar tissue inside it was hard to stop the bleeding."

"Scar tissue? Why would she have scar tissue on her insides?"

"Well from the file we have here at the ER, your wife was brought in over a year ago with a massive hemorrhage."

"Excuse me!" I moved over to Cazi because I could see him getting angry.

"Yea she mentioned having an abortion and not feeling good. By the time she got here it was so much blood we had to give her a transfusion because she almost died." Yariah covered her mouth and Aphrodite didn't know what to say.

"When was this again?" The doctor looked at the file and gave him a date. I knew then Amara was in some deep shit.

"Is her scarring the reason we're having problems conceiving?"

"Most likely but I'm not her gynecologist so I can't say for sure."

"Wait! The doctor told us we didn't have anything wrong and it would take time to have kids."

"Technically, there isn't a problem besides the scar tissue. If you went to a doctor and they told you it wasn't, then he or she may not have known her history. That, or even though you were there with her, the doctor didn't reveal her medical history due to privacy." Cazi nodded and I saw the steam coming out his ears if that's even possible.

"Back to the subject at hand. Your wife is going to need extensive therapy and continuous support when she goes home. I suggest hiring a nurse and being as strong for her as possible."

"Yup." Is all Cazi said.

"Would you like to see her?"

"Yea."

"Go with him Caleek."

"You know I love y'all, but I need to see her alone. I promise not to address anything right now. Well, I'll try." He walked in the back and said he'll be out when she wakes up and we could stay or not.

"You ready to go?"

"Yea. Caleek we need to talk at the house." I handed her the phone and purse.

"About?"

"Let's talk there. I don't want everyone in our business." I guess its time to tell him about the pregnancy. I won't be happy carrying at the same time as Lori, but we should've been protected.

"Aight but it has to be after I make up."

"And that you definitely have to do." She stood on her tippy toes to kiss me.

"We're gonna go too." Aphrodite said and walked over with Bongi. The two of them have been together almost everyday. I have to say, its good to see him smiling after the shit he's been through with his baby mama.

"So what y'all a big happy family now?" I turned, and Lori was standing there grinning.

"Caleek you can handle her." I could see the aggravation on Yariah's face.

"Lori what's really good? I told you to stop coming for my sister." Lori threw her head back laughing. When did she start defending Yariah to Lori?

"Your sister huh?" Ro started taking her earrings off. Bongi was holding her back. He told her his woman wasn't about to be fighting like some hood rat and he'd make sure someone off the street beat her ass. I didn't even care he threatened her because she deserved it. I'm gonna tell him later to have it done after she delivers. If that's my child I don't want anything to happen to him or her.

"Was she your sister when you were sending naked flicks and nasty ass text messages to my man?" Yariah and Bongi looked at Aphrodite. How the hell did the bitch even know because I damn sure ain't tell?

"Begging to suck his dick and you promised to keep y'all fake ass love affair a secret."

"Yo, you tried to fuck my boy? What type of shit you on?"

"Bongi it wasn't like that and..." Ro was mad as shit and tryna explain.

"And what sis? You know how long we've been feeling each other, and you were tryna fuck him. I could see if I did it to you." Now my girl was getting upset.

"Riah it was a while ago and Bongi we never fucked."

"That's not the damn point. How I know you not fucking me to be around him?" He was mad as hell and I don't blame him. I wouldn't wanna be with a chick who was feeling one of my boys either.

"Bongi, I don't want him. Don't let her make you think I'm with you for any other reason than what it is."

"Caleek why didn't you tell me?" I wasn't saying anything. I stared at Lori getting enjoyment once again outta hurting Yariah.

"This ain't the time Riah. Hold on."

"What you mean it ain't the time? I just found out my sisters was tryna fuck you. We're best friends and you should've told me. Why were you hiding it?" I heard the disappointment in her voice. I picked my phone up that was ringing in my pocket.

"Caleek where you at? I got some news." I used my index finger and pressed down on one ear to hear the detective.

"I'm at the hospital. What's up?"

"Stay there. I'm getting ready to pull in."

"I'm about to leave." I saw Riah walking to the door and grabbed her wrist.

"Whatever it is can it wait until tomorrow?" I felt her tryna break loose and gave her a look to relax.

"We found Tasheem's body." I let go and walked off a little.

"Where?"

"Hold on. I'm here." He disconnected the call and I told Riah we were about to leave. She acted like she wasn't leaving, but she was wrong because her ass is coming home with me and we about to discuss this shit.

"You fucking bitch." Ro started beating the shit outta Lori. Bongi stood there with his head against the wall in deep thought. He just told us the other day he thinks Aphrodite is the one. Don't ask me how when they've only been messing a few months, but I guess when you know, you know.

"Break it up." Security came running up and struggled to pull them apart.

"Caleek did you sleep with my sister?" I pulled Riah close and kissed her neck and then lips.

"Never. If we didn't get together, I still wouldn't have done it"

"Why didn't you tell me then?"

"Caleek." I turned around and there was the agent and two officers.

"Hey." We slapped hands and I turned to see the aggravation and hurt on Riah's face. I was gonna tell her everything when we got to the house, but I had to deal with this first.

"Like I told you on the phone. We found her."

"Was she badly burned?"

"See for yourself." He stepped out the way and the door opened.

"OH MY GOD!" Riah shouted and everyone looked in our direction. Well I thought they did because it seemed to get quiet and I felt like all eyes were on me.

"What the fuck?" I moved towards the door and Tasheem was standing there crying.

"How the... where have you been?" I hugged her tight and didn't wanna let her go.

"Are you Ms. Yariah Perry?" I turned around after asking if she were ok and where has she been all this time.

"Yes." The cop took his handcuffs out and walked behind her.

"Yo, what the hell you doing?"

"Caleek she's the reason I was gone for so long." Tasheem shouted and I stared at Riah, then Tasheem and back to Riah. *What the fuck was going on?*

"Huh?"

"You're under arrest for the kidnapping and abduction of Tasheem Compton. You're also under arrest for the murder of four other people in a warehouse outside of town as well as arson."

"What?" I shouted and ran over to Riah. Ro was tryna console Riah who appeared upset but the look she gave me was crazy.

"Riah tell me right now that they're bugging." I couldn't even begin to believe Yariah would do something like this.

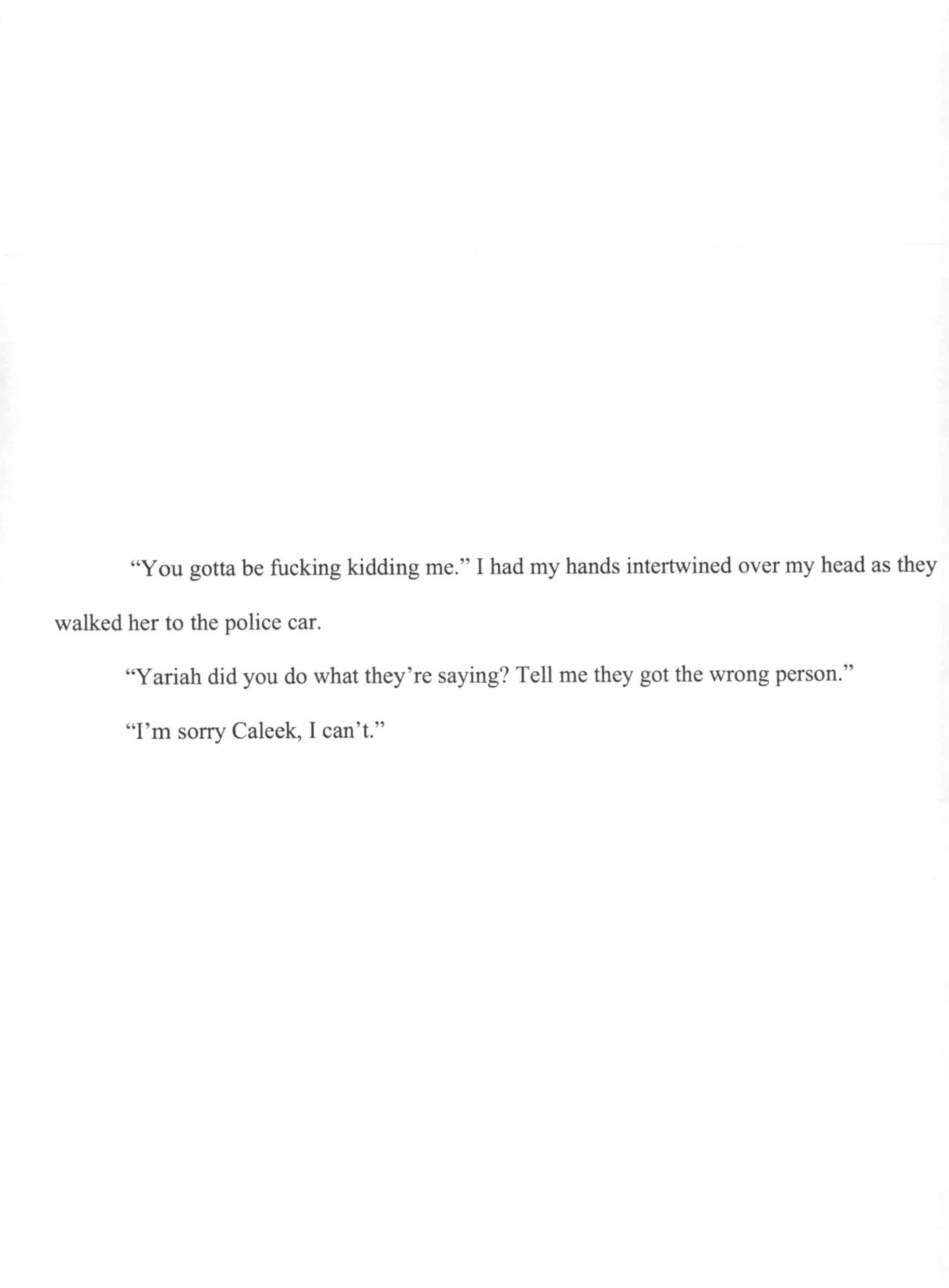

"You gotta be fucking kidding me." I had my hands intertwined over my head as they walked her to the police car.

"Yariah did you do what they're saying? Tell me they got the wrong person."

"I'm sorry Caleek, I can't."

***At the hospital…***

## *Caleek*

"Tha fuck you mean you can't?" I barked at Yariah before the officer stopped to open the car door. All of a sudden, cameras began flashing and paparazzi came outta nowhere. How the hell did they get here and how did they even know?

"Caleek, I can't tell you anything because I don't know what's going on. Please don't let me sit in jail." Tears were racing down her face.

"Caleek you better not go get her. She kept me locked away for almost two years. We lost our baby because of what she did." Tasheem yelled behind my back. The way Yariah stared at her did something to me. Was she tryna reveal something with her eyes or was she mad at Tasheem for telling? I was at a loss for words right now.

"You know what Caleek?"

"Riah, I'll be there." I put my hands on her face and kissed her lips. Regardless of Tasheem being safe and alive I still wanted Yariah.

"No, she's right Leek. You've missed her, and I know it took a lot outta you to move on. Now she's back and you two deserve each other. Go live your happy ever after."

"Officer why are you allowing her to speak to my man? She should be on her way to rot in jail." The officer nodded, put his hand on Riah's head and helped her in the car. I watched them drive off before directing my attention to Tasheem and these reporters.

"We're live at the hospital where a woman who was declared deceased almost two years ago reunited with the love of her life. But the twist in this story is, he's moved on and the woman is the exact person who's responsible for her disappearance. How do you feel sir?"

"Bitch get that camera and microphone out my face." I mushed her and the rest of the people out the way. I placed my hand on the small of Tasheem back and led her in the hospital. She seemed to be enjoying the spectacle, where I'm pissed.

"Caleek let me speak to you for a minute." Agent Hart pulled me in a corner and Tasheem followed. By the look on his face I don't think he wanted her to hear.

"I'm glad to see she's back safe."

"Oh my God Tasheem! How is this even possible?" Her mom cried running in the hospital.

"Who called your family?" If they just found her, how was she able to contact anyone? Better yet, why didn't she contact me first or come looking for me?

"I did on the way over." She kissed my cheek and went to where they were.

"Watch your back." I snapped my neck.

"Keep a smile on your face and pretend we're enjoying their reunion." I turned and did like he asked.

"This entire story is suspect as shit and I don't think your girl had anything to do with it."

"Yariah doesn't have it in her to do this." We spoke through gritted teeth.

"No but this one has already hired one of the top attorneys in the state to represent her." I turned. I didn't care if she knew we were speaking about her.

"She's trying to get the death penalty for Yariah and she's suing the owner where the warehouse was located."

"Are you serious?"

"As a heart attack. Stop by the office when you get a chance. There's more to this story and a whole lotta shit missing too." He gave me a pound and walked out the door.

"Caleek did you tell Lori about the text messages and videos?" Ro asked as she walked up on me. I noticed Bongi step off when they placed Yariah in handcuffs.

"Get the fuck out my face with that shit Ro. You of all people should know I'd never purposely hurt Riah."

"Then how did she get it?"

"I can't focus on that right now." I noticed Lori in the corner with a confused look on her face too but why? The bitch caused mad drama before any of this Tasheem crap happened.

"Caleek, I know it's a lot to ask but can you please talk to Bongi?" She grabbed my arm and I gave her a look to let go.

"What the fuck am I supposed to say?" I folded my arms and stared down at her. I still had eyes on Lori in one corner and Tasheem being extra with her family in the other.

"I don't know but I'm in love with him. Please." I saw how watery her eyes were getting.

"A'ight. I'm only doing it because you're gonna do the same and tell Yariah the truth about your fake ass crush too."

"Fine!" She had the nerve to catch an attitude.

"Kill that attitude and take yo ass down to the station to get her."

"Are they going to give her a bail and why aren't you going?" I gave her a dumb ass look.

"I'm gonna be there shortly." I glanced over at Tasheem.

"Caleek, I know I'm the last person you care to hear from but we both know my sister had nothing to do with Tasheem's disappearance or whatever it is she's accusing her of." I ran my hand over my face.

"I know but the real question running through my head is why did Tasheem do it?"

"She faked her own death?" Ro asked a question I wanted to know my damn self.

"I don't know but she had some sort of involvement. There's no way…" I stopped speaking when Tasheem headed towards us.

"Go get your sister and tell her I'll be by later." She nodded and rushed out the hospital.

"Hey baby. I missed you so much." She tried to kiss me and I turned my head.

"I'll be back."

"Where you going?" She had a snarl on her face.

"I need to let Cazi know what's going on. Wait here." I asked the receptionist to allow me access to the back and went to Amara's room. Cazi had his head on the bed holding her hand. I didn't wanna disturb him but this shit is important.

"How she doing?" He lifted his head and I could tell he had been crying.

"She's alive and to me, it's all that matters. What's up?" He used the back of his hand to wipe the few tears.

"How long before she wakes up?"

"It could be tonight or tomorrow. The doctor said the medication was pretty strong."

"Oh ok. We need to talk real quick."

"You good?" He asked me to close the door in Amara's room. I made sure no one was coming and started explaining the shit going on. He was as shocked as me and even more pissed Tasheem named Yariah as the culprit who made her disappear.

"What you gonna do?"

"I had Ro go get her and I'm sure your pops will be there." He left right after they told us what happened with Amara so he missed everything.

"I'm gonna take Tasheem home and find out what the fuck happened."

"Listen bro, I know shit is crazy right now but don't leave my sister hanging. If you're gonna make it work with Tasheem then let her go and I mean really let her go."

"That's the thing. When Tasheem showed up of course I was surprised but none of my feelings came back. I walked Riah to the police car and kissed her in front of Tasheem. I still only want her."

"I get it and you know I stay outta your love life but Tasheem ain't about to let that slide. She's gonna wanna pick up where she left off and Riah won't stick around for anymore bullshit." I felt like he was talking in code. It's like he knew something I didn't.

I ain't even tryna be with Tasheem and I was low key pissed when Yariah told me to live happy ever after with her. She knows like everyone else how much I want her.

We've been through a lot to be together and I'm not hiding my relationship or feelings for no one; not even my ex who came back from the dead. Damn, do I even call her my ex because she died, and we weren't broken up? All I know is I'm not pushing Yariah aside for her or anyone else.

"I'll hit you up later."

"A'ight. I'm gonna call Aphrodite and see if Riah has a bail or anything." He said and grabbed his phone off the bed.

"I sent a text to our lawyer so he's on his way there. You know she won't be there long."

"Good looking out and we'll meet up to discuss the other shit." He pointed to the door where Tasheem was standing.

"Bro, if she comes in here, I'll probably knock her the fuck out." I busted out laughing. I wasn't even mad he threatened her. That's how I know I'm over Tasheem. I'd never allow anyone to talk shit about her, not even him or her family.

****************************

"It feels so good to be home. I missed you Caleek." Tasheem wrapped her arms around my neck when we stepped out the car.

"You missed me so much that you contacted the media, cops, your family and a lawyer before me?" She removed her hands and stepped back.

"Caleek it's not what you think."

"Then you need to tell me because none of this makes any sense."

"What doesn't make sense is your perfect Yariah kidnapping me and holding me hostage." I chuckled because she sounded stupid as fuck.

"How the hell did she pull it off? I mean Cazi showed up at the warehouse and no one was there besides us." I asked.

Cazi told me when they got to the warehouse and knocked the doors down, there were a few people there. They couldn't see who they were due to the gunfire. However; he did say a car sped off with two people inside; per the video surveillance but you couldn't see who they were. The video footage from the warehouse didn't show much but the ones from a store a mile away did show the car, the license plate and two people.

He called me to his office and had me look but again, nothing about them were recognizable. The license plate went back to some old ass couple who reported their car stolen the same night. By the time it was recovered, someone burned it. We figured it was to kill any DNA and any other things the cops may find. We left it alone and started looking into other things. But not once did I suspect Yariah and I still don't. The two of them may not have gotten along but Riah don't even fuck with people so where would she get a team to do this?

"Stop underestimating the things the bitch is capable of." She rolled her eyes and I snatched her up.

"One thing you won't do is call her a bitch." I had her against the car with her shirt balled up in my hand.

"Caleek you've never put your hands on me." I let her go and backed away.

"Maybe its best if you stay with your parents." I hit the alarm on the truck to unlock it. We were on our way in the house and she started popping shit, I can only imagine what else is gonna happen. To avoid it, it's best we stay in separate houses.

"All this time away from me and you still wanna be apart?" I saw her getting teary eyed.

"Tasheem you have no idea what I'm feeling right now. I mean you're supposed to be dead and yet, you're standing in front of me alive and well. Then, you're claiming the woman you hate the most is responsible."

"I understand Caleek because I wouldn't know what to do either. I wouldn't push you away though."

"Look. Just stay with your parents tonight and I'll pick you up in the morning. We can go to breakfast and you can tell me everything."

"Let me guess. You're going to her?"

"Whether you stayed here tonight or not, I was still going to her." I opened the truck door and waited for her to get in.

"I can't believe you're going to see the woman who kept us apart." She pouted and plopped in the seat with her arms folded. I sat on the driver's side and pulled out the driveway.

"The same way I'm gonna hear you out, I'm gonna do the same for her." I stopped at the light and turned her face to me. I used my thumb to wipe the tears coming down her face. As bad as I wanted to show affection or even love on her, I couldn't. Something wasn't right and until I heard from Riah, I won't put myself in a fucked-up situation. I did it once with Lori and Riah left me alone. I'm not tryna lose her again.

"We're gonna get through this Tasheem and if it comes out Yariah is the one responsible, we'll deal with it." I continued driving when the light changed with a bunch of thoughts running through my mind.

"I'll pick you up in the morning." I parked in front of her parent's place. It was a lotta people out there including the guy she fucked around with on our break. I didn't even have the energy to address it.

"I don't know why he's here Caleek." I nodded and kissed her cheek. Who the fuck she think she fooling?

"Tomorrow morning."

"K." She closed the door and started accepting the hugs from everyone. I drove off and to the police station.

# *Yariah*

"Turn to the right." The woman cop shouted. I turned and heard the camera click.

"Turn to the left." I repeated the step and then faced forward. Not only was I being arrested for a crime I didn't commit, I now had a mug shot. I'm gonna be in databases throughout law enforcement agencies. My fingerprints will be floating around everywhere.

"Ok. This way." The woman looped her hand around my arm and guided me in another room.

The handcuffs were still around my wrists and they were so tight I knew my circulation was cut off. Let alone my tears were dried up on my cheeks, snot was probably in my hair because pieces were stuck on my face and my throat was dry as hell. I asked the officer for something to drink and I'm still waiting.

You would think after doing the paperwork I'd be offered a seat or something. This particular cop had me standing the entire time and when I asked to pee, she stood at the door to watch me. I couldn't even wipe correctly because she refused to unhook one handcuff. I would call her petty, but she doesn't know me to be that way.

"Take your clothes off and turn around."

"Hold up."

"Hold up what?" She stood over me with her body. This woman had to be a good 350 pounds with a gut she probably has to lift to use the bathroom. You know the kind that hangs almost to your knees. How the hell she's a cop is beyond me. I mean who's she gonna run down?

"I may be new to this, but I know damn well I'm not supposed to strip. Now if I go to the county or a prison that's a different story."

"You heard what the fuck I said." She barked and tried to intimidate me with her stared down.

"And you heard what the fuck I said. I'm not stripping."

*WHAP!* She smacked me so hard, my body fell against the wall.

"Oh no you didn't." I had to catch my balance to keep from hitting the wall.

"Yes I did." This bitch cracked her neck and her knuckles. I ain't never been scared of no one and I'm not about to be now.

I ran up on her and did a high kick in her face. She tumbled back and fell in the chair. I started punching her in the face over and over until I felt my body being lifted.

"Ms. Perry, you continue to add charges, don't you?"

"Hell no. You saw her fat ass hit me on that camera right there." I pointed to the small one they had hidden in the corner. My brother and Leek told me to always check my surroundings for cameras. You can find the smallest ones in the cracks of walls, which is where they had one.

"What's going on and why does my client have a swollen face?" The cop remained quiet.

"I'd say we'll call this incident even." The lawyer smirked at the cop who was struggling to get up.

"She assaulted an officer."

"And by the looks of things, I'd say she was defending herself. You can file a charge if you'd like but we both know it won't go anywhere once I sue the shit outta this precinct for attacking innocent people."

"Innocent? This bitch ain't innocent." The cop started to walk towards me and the lawyer blocked her.

"She already whooped your ass. You may wanna get that eye looked at." I cracked a smile and the bitch had the nerve to threaten me.

"Strike two. If you make one more threat or attempt to attack her, I'll make sure you get fired and evicted from your place. Don't play with me officer Jones." He looked at her badge.

"What's going on in here?"

"Hey captain. We had a little situation, but it's handled. Isn't that right Ms. Jones?" Her face was turned up.

"Yes."

"What happened to your face?" The captain questioned her.

"Nothing." She stormed out and so did the other officer who thought he would charge me with assault.

"Let's speak in the conference room." We followed him out and he closed the door.

"Usually I don't get involved because there's people assigned to this case, but I received a call that she's the sister of Cazi Perry and the girlfriend of Caleek Simms." I rolled my eyes.

"What I'm trying to figure out is how she's involved." He continued talking.

"She's not; which is why I'm here. What do we need to do in order for her to be released?"

"I've spoken with the judge already and because this has become a media frenzy, she's gonna have to pay a bail."

"What you mean?" I asked confused.

"Because Tasheem Compton made a spectacle outta this, we have to do things by the book. The bail is set at two million dollars with no ten percent. It has to be in cash and you can't leave the state or country."

"Are you serious?" I responded with attitude.

"Unfortunately, I am."

"Ms. Perry don't worry about it. The bail has already been paid." My lawyer told me and took some papers out his briefcase.

"How? He just told me the price and I haven't been able to contact anyone."

"Just because you didn't know, doesn't mean we weren't already working on it." He winked, and I sat there listening to all the bullshit Tasheem accused me of. The charges were ridiculous and so was the amount of time each one held. All he did is aggravate me more.

"Can I go?" If he's my lawyer, then I don't heed to listen. He'll let me know later.

"Yes. Stay outta trouble." The captain joked and put his hand out for me to shake. I snatched the door open and walked out.

"I'm sorry Ms. Perry." I heard and turned around to see the cop bitch standing next to Caleek with tears running down her face.

"What?"

"I apologize for disrespecting and laying hands on you."

"What the hell you crying for?" I asked because she wasn't upset a little while ago when she was popping shit. I looked down and he had her hand in his. It appeared that he was squeezing the shit out of it.

"Keep going." Caleek barked.

"If you need anything please call me."

"Caleek what's going on?" I covered my mouth when he smashed her face in the wall. Her body fell, and you could tell her nose was broken.

"Nothing. You ready?" He took my hand in his and escorted me out the police station.

"You ok?" He checked me over and leaned me against the truck.

"I'm fine. Take me home please."

"I am." His index finger went under my chin for me look at him.

"I know you didn't do this and we're gonna get through it." His lips crashed against mine and the two of us stood there kissing. If someone didn't clear their throat we'd probably still be there.

"The first hearing is next week. Make sure she attends." Caleek shook the lawyers' hand and thanked him. The lawyer walked off and left us staring at one another.

"Get in." He said and help me inside.

"Yariah, I swear on my life that I'm gonna find out what's really going on."

"Leek maybe you should distance yourself from me." He started the truck.

"Why would I do that?"

"What if you can't find the truth? What if whoever did this had help and covered up their tracks? I don't wanna go to jail." I started crying hysterically. I felt the car pull over to the side and his truck door open.

"Come here." He pulled me out and hugged me tight.

"You will never step foot in a jail cell."

"Caleek we don't know what's going on and..."

"And I'm gonna find out the truth. I won't ever allow my future wife and mother of my kids to sit in jail." I stared and saw all the sincerity in his face and voice. Should I mention the pregnancy? No, I'll wait just in case I decide to get rid of it. I'm not raising my child from prison. I know he says he'll figure it out but what if he doesn't?

After hugging me again, he had me get back in and drove to my house. My father and sister were waiting. You could tell they'd been crying, and I felt bad. My dad hugged me tight and so did Ro. I know I'm supposed to be angry with her right now, but I just don't have the energy. I told them we could talk tomorrow because I needed to rest.

"It's easier said than done but baby try to stop stressing." Caleek whispered in my ear as he unhooked my bra. He helped me finish getting undressed, started a bath and got in with me. It definitely relaxed me, and I appreciated him being here. I also know he's gonna have a lotta issues dealing with Tasheem. I hope he can find the truth in the process.

# *Tasheem*

“Why the fuck were you with him?” Tone asked when I stepped out the truck. Why the hell is he questioning me anyway?

Tone is the guy I dated when Caleek and I broke up. He was the man I cried too, and the one I slept with to hurt Caleek. Yea it was petty and childish but in the midst of it, I started catching feelings for him, yet my heart remained with Leek. I knew no other man could take his place and didn’t try to see if anyone could.

Over the four-month span Tone and I were together, he became more possessive and wanted to be my man. I couldn’t comply with his demand because I knew I’d get back with Leek; it’s what we did. We’d break up for a few months and get back together.

Tone started threatening to tell everyone about the affair, but it didn’t matter because by that time, Leek and I were on speaking terms and knew of him. He said once we got back together, I had to lose all contact with Tone and I had no problem listening.

Somehow; Tone became close with my brother and started hating Caleek for no reason at all. Granted, he wanted me to be his woman but other than that he had no legit issue with Leek.

He started doing petty shit like texting me in the middle if the night to make Leek think it was more than it was. He’d show up at the grocery store if we weren’t together tryna make me see he’s the right man for me. I had to block him from everything and stopped visiting my parents if Luther was there. He too would be childish and invite Tone over if I stopped by.

My brother couldn’t stand Caleek for his own reasons too. He was given a job and fucked it up. I tried to go to bat for him with Leek, but he wasn’t having it. He said Luther stole from him, had some of his most loyal employees on board that he fired and cost him a lotta money. I couldn't argue but I did when he almost beat him to death over it.

Now that I think about it, Leek beat his ass a few times. Luther wanted me to save him and like I said, I tried but he ran his mouth too much and Leek wasn't having it. He knew like everyone else in the streets the type of man Leek is and pushed his luck. Tone felt his wrath once too at the mall because he was being smart and got his ass whooped. I couldn't even feel bad.

"Tone right now is not the time." My father spoke and grabbed my hand to go inside. My brother was on the couch with some chick and my mom came rushing out the kitchen.

"If I knew you were coming home tonight, I would've cooked a big dinner."

"It's ok ma. Is my room still the same?" She had a concerned look on her face.

"Let me show you." I followed her up the steps and when she opened the door it was exactly the same as I left it.

Before all this happened, I stayed with Caleek, but my mom kept my room. She always told me that there's a place for me here if I ever wanted to return. The bed had the same comforters, the curtains, TV and the towels I used were still all the same. I'm all for keeping things original but damn.

"Why are you here honey?" She asked and closed the door.

"He went to her." I started crying. She sat next to me and I placed my head on her shoulder.

"Tasheem I'm about to say something and I don't care if you get upset." I lifted my head and wiped my eyes.

"When you passed or was kidnapped Caleek didn't run to her." I gave her a *yea right* look.

"I'm serious. I may not be in the streets, but I know for a fact he wasn't."

"I bet she was around."

"Yes she was but he started screwing any and everyone."

"Huh?"

"He was distraught after you passed. He wasn't trying to get in a relationship until this other woman came around. From what his mom tells me, Caleek and Yariah just made it official."

"Really? And you speak to his mom?" I questioned because why would they still be conversing if I'm supposedly dead?

"Really and she called me once a month to ask how I was doing. Tasheem look." She stood in front of me.

"I know you think Caleek should welcome you back with open arms but he's a different man now."

"But I'm still me."

"Yes, but I'm sure you returning has him trying to figure out what's going on too."

"That's the thing. I don't know what happened."

"You mean to tell me, this entire time you had no idea what was going on?" I could understand why she was skeptical on believing me but its the truth. I had no idea what happened to me.

"I'll tell you the story tomorrow. I'm tired right now and I have to figure out a way to get my man back."

"Tasheem I'm just going to say this once."

"What?" I took my shirt off and grabbed a towel.

"Leave that man alone."

"Ma, he's my fiancé." Why would she even think I'd be ok with not tryna get my man back.

"Ex Tasheem."

"WE NEVER BROKE UP. I WAS KIDNAPPED!" I shouted, and my mom jumped.

"Don't you scream at me."

"I'm sorry mommy. It's just, how can he be happy with someone else and I'm alive?" She shook her head.

"Everyone thought you we're dead Tasheem. Did you expect him to stop his life?"

"I would've."

"I find that hard to believe." She rolled her eyes.

"And why is that?"

"Luther told us your little secret about the baby and how you were pregnant by Tone."

"I wasn't pregnant by Tone." She opened the door and there he was standing in the doorway.

"Whatever you say." She moved past him, and he stepped in.

"How are you?" Tone asked and sat on my bed.

"Fine. Give me a minute." I shut the bathroom door, turned the shower on and stepped in.

I didn't bother wiping the tears cascading down my face as I stood there thinking about how two years of my life was stolen. I don't care what anyone says, Yariah had everything to do with my abduction and I'm gonna expose her for the fraud she is.

I never had an issue with her until I noticed how attentive Caleek was to her once she turned 17. I used to see her all the time due to Leek being best friends with Cazi. She was always a pretty girl but the minute she started developing more, I could see the crush she had on Leek. It may have been there, but she never made it noticeable.

I would've never thought anything of it had she not started flirting with him in my face. She'd come in the room we were in and sit next to him and they'd have their own conversation. I'd watch as she would push on his arm if he said something funny or be extra with her laugh. Amara told me I was looking too far into it and so did Leek, and maybe I was but regardless of it being a crush I knew something was up.

Anyway, Leek began to spend more time over there and when I asked why he didn't bring me like usual, it was always, *oh I wasn't there long, or he just dropped something off.* I found out later it was more with them because I walked in one day and they were in the kitchen being extra friendly. Neither of them knew of my presence and continued laughing and joking about stupid shit.

I can't even remember what was said, but Leek moved closer to her and ran his hand down her face. The look he gave her was of pure love and no matter how much I didn't wanna admit it, I knew I was losing him. All the breaking up and getting back together was taking a toll on our relationship.

I cleared my throat and he backed away. I played it off as if I didn't see what was going on, but my heart was aching at the sight. From that day on I told him he couldn't go over there without me. I wasn't tryna run him, but I planned on making him fall back in love with me and it worked because he proposed.

I accepted and couldn't be happier, that is until I watched her follow him to the bathroom at my party. He didn't ask her too or give out any signals, but I guess she decided to do what she wanted. I heard her congratulate him and he went in after her. Before anything could happen, I busted in. You damn right I tried to get him to fuck me in there. Yariah needed to know he was mine and to back off. I wanted her to hear me moaning out his name and him letting her know how good our sex life was.

Unfortunately, he had us go in a closet to fuck. It wasn't the same as her hearing, but she knew we fucked because when we came back her face was turned up. I was overjoyed seeing her hurt over him moving on from whatever she thought they were gonna have.

Leek and I had been together for years and no young heffa was coming in to take what we've built. I guess she wanted him badly because she made me disappear by any means necessary and now look; the bitch got him and she's pregnant. Yea, I noticed he small pouch in her stomach. I'm assuming it's his because she did have a man before this happened. I don't think Leek knew she was because he would've mentioned it when he said he was going to get her. Its gonna really take some proof to make him see she's not the picture-perfect woman he assumed she was, but I'm gonna do it or at least try.

"What are you doing?" I questioned Tone when he stepped in the shower behind me.

"I missed you Sheemy."

"How could you miss someone you hated?" I asked him because the last time he tried to reach out before this happened, he claimed to hate me.

"I never hated you. Did I want you as my own? Absolutely but I've never hated or wished bad luck on you." He made me face him.

"I was devastated when they said you died in an explosion." I could tell how hurt he was, but it doesn't explain why he's in the shower with me or why I'm allowing him to fondle me.

"Tone this isn't right." I tried to move his hand, but he wouldn't budge.

"I wanted to die too. I missed you so much baby." He was pouring it on thick to me.

"Sssssss. I have a man and oh shit…" I cried out in pleasure when he made me cum on his hand.

"That nigga you claiming is with his bitch." I pushed him off and told him to get out. What's his purpose of bringing the shit up.

"I ain't going nowhere." He lifted me in his arms and rammed himself inside.

"Tone." I moaned out and dug my nails in his back. Is this rape because I didn't tell him to enter me? Yet, the way he has my body succumbing to these orgasms isn't make me stop him.

"Fuck that nigga Sheemy. It's me and you." Two years of no sex, it felt like he was ripping me open. He pumped harder and had me almost screaming.

After cumming so much, he washed us both up, carried me in the room and passed out next to me. As bad as I didn't wanna say it, I needed that.

## *Yariah*

"How you feeling sweetie?" My dad pulled me away from the stove and embraced me in a hug. I started crying again and rested my head on his chest.

"Does she hate me that much daddy? Why else would she make those accusations against me?" He moved me away to look at him.

"Jealousy and envy are the most dangerous things a woman can feel when it comes to what she considers hers."

"Tasheem isn't ugly and why would she envy me?"

"You have the man she's tried to keep away from you all these years. Did you expect her not to assume you were the one who kidnapped her?"

"But why me and she didn't even know about Caleek and I."

"That's what you think?" He winked and picked up a piece of bacon off the plate.

"If she arrived at the hospital with cops, news stations and whoever else, trust me she's been back." Is it possible? Could she have returned sooner and not let anyone know?

"Why wouldn't she make herself known?"

"She was too busy tryna make you take the fall."

"Well it worked because I damn sure went through the system last night." My father chuckled.

"Then I get into it with the big Bertha chick of a cop. Daddy she was huge." I snickered thinking about the high kick I gave her and Caleek knocking her into the wall. I don't condone a man hitting a woman but sometimes it's hard not to.

"Caleek told me a little about what happened."

"When?" I questioned because I had no clue they spoke.

"Last night."

"Last night. I didn't even know he got out the bed."

"I came to check on you because I thought he left, and he got up. He said you were tossing and turning for two hours and finally went to sleep. I asked what exactly went down at the hospital and he told me." He continued talking as I turned the stove off and started making a plate for us.

I slept off and on throughout the night and the last time I woke up, I decided to cook breakfast. It's the least I could do for Caleek after he rescued me from Lock up.

"Honey, the cop deserved it for putting her hands on you." He said and walked over to make his own plate.

"Do you think I'm going to jail?"

"Nope and you know why?" My father was very confident in his response.

"Why?"

"Because your brother or Caleek won't allow it."

"OH MY GOD! I forgot all about Amara. Is she ok?" I shouted, and he jumped from me scaring him.

"She's fine Riah. Cazi is good too and trying to find a way to ask why she had an abortion or something. When was she pregnant?" He was confused as all of us were when the doctor mentioned it. I explained what I could assume happened and that's, that Amara became pregnant and terminated it.

“You think it was Cazi baby?” I know he asked because of how close Amara and I are but she never told me anything about it. I wonder if it’s what she wanted to speak about before the accident.

“I can’t even tell you.”

“Riah?” My dad called out on my way up the steps with the food.

“Yea.” I slightly turned. I didn’t wanna drop our food.

“You need to tell him.”

“I know daddy.”

“He’ll keep you safe and right now you need to be protected.”

“I promise to tell him.” He smiled and walked back in the kitchen.

When I got upstairs and opened the door, Leek was laying in the bed on the phone. I couldn’t help but stare at his bare chest and the print under the sheet. My man had a dick the same size of a porn star.

If I had to compare him to anyone it would definitely be Rico Star. That man’s dick is extremely big, and he be fucking the shit outta those women. Leek is exactly the same and I must say, he may disable my uterus at times but it’s worth it.

“A’ight. I’ll be there in a few.” I walked over and handed him his plate and juice. I sat my food on the nightstand and went to the bathroom.

“Look at my wife cooking for me.” He said when I came out and picked up a piece of toast.

“Leek, I have to tell you something.”

“Can it wait, or do you need to tell me because I got something to tell you?” He seemed to be excited about whatever it is. I hope he has the same energy when I reveal my pregnancy.

"You go first." I told him and smiled.

"The house I had built from the ground up for us, is complete."

"What?" I couldn't have been hearing him correctly.

"I said." He moved the plate over and had me sit down in front of him.

"Yariah Perry, I always knew we'd be together."

"Caleek you were with Tasheem and y'all were gonna get married."

"I'm not just saying this because of how things played out, but Riah I would've never made it down the aisle." I covered my mouth in shock.

"I was in love with her at one point in my life but once you stole my heart, she couldn't retrieve it back no matter how hard she tried. I believe you are my soulmate Yariah and that's real talk." He pulled me in for a kiss.

"As far as the house goes, it's been in the making for over a year." He picked his plate back up to finish eating.

"A year?" I asked. Who knew he's been planning for us to be together even with Lori in his life.

"I wanted everything to be perfect for you, which is why your brother and Amara had a hand in helping me design it." I busted out crying.

"What the hell is up with you and all this crying?" He wiped my eyes.

"Leek, I'm..."

*KNOCK! KNOCK!* We both looked at the door.

"Riah can we talk?" Aphrodite shouted.

"For what?"

"Please." Ro begged and I so didn't feel like being bothered.

"Go ahead babe. Y'all need this." He stuffed the last forkful of eggs in his mouth and leaned over to get his clothes.

"But I don't wanna." I pouted and sat against the headboard.

"If you hear her out, I promise to make you scream later."

"And I promise to make you moan." I crawled over to the edge where he was standing to put his jeans on.

"You're the only one who can." I smirked and stood on the bed.

"I'm gonna have to do something extra special if you're buying me houses and stuff." I rested my hands on his shoulders.

"I'll buy you whatever you want Yariah Simms." I giggled like a schoolgirl when he added his name at the end.

"I love you Leek." He had me step off the bed and embraced me.

"I love you more than I can say and nothing or nobody is gonna split us up again." His hands gripped my ass and mine were sliding under his shirt. I loved touching his body.

"Call me when you're finished with her. I wanna take you to see the house." He smacked me on the ass.

"Really?" I was excited to finally be moving into my own place. I could've left a long time ago but after my mom went into rehab I didn't wanna leave my dad alone.

"Yup." He walked to the door.

"Oh babe. What did you have to tell me?" He stopped before opening it.

"I'll tell you later."

"A'ight and no fighting." He pecked my lips again and opened the door. Ro was standing there biting her nail.

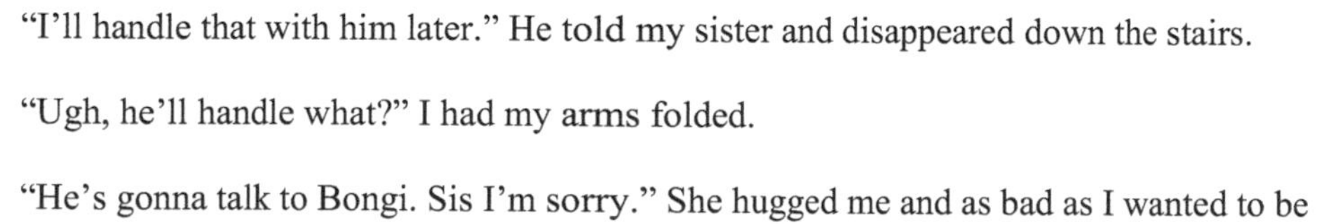

"I'll handle that with him later." He told my sister and disappeared down the stairs.

"Ugh, he'll handle what?" I had my arms folded.

"He's gonna talk to Bongi. Sis I'm sorry." She hugged me and as bad as I wanted to be mad, I couldn't be. If anything happened between them, I probably would but a crush is just a crush. I am going to discuss the messages and videos tho.

"Let me take a shower and then we can talk." She nodded, and I left her standing there. I hope whatever she's about to say doesn't piss me off.

## *Aphrodite*

"I'm listening." Yariah said when she emerged from the bathroom.

"Ok. I used to have a crush on Leek." She sucked her teeth.

"It happened a couple of years ago when I broke up with Samuel." Riah continued to walk around the room getting dressed.

"I don't know why I gained this crush knowing you two were feeling one another." She stopped moving and looked at me.

"To be honest, I think it's because he reminded me so much of Samuel. I wanted him back so bad I latched on to the person who resembled him."

Samuel is my ex from college and the two of us were together the entire time we attended. Him and Caleek had a lotta similarities and yet weren't related. They had the same build, complexion and some of their ways were easy to compare. I never meant to have a crush on the same person as my sister and it kinda just happened.

Anyway, Samuel cheated on me heavy. I mean it was so bad his fiancé came to the campus tryna fight me. Yes, his fiancé. Come to find out they had been engaged for a year and we were already a couple for three. How he did that is beyond me, but they say a man can live a double life. It's crazy because I met his family and even attended holiday parties with him and other functions. He was good as hell hiding it.

Long story short, even after learning of the fiancé, my dumb ass stayed because he claimed to have broken things off and it would be about us. We went to couples counseling and everything. Who knew this nigga had a two-year-old and a baby on the way? That was the last straw and I finally freed myself from him.

One day I was in my feelings and drinking at the club. Caleek came in and it's like Samuel took over my brain. When I saw Caleek, I saw my ex. I was devastated over the split and sadly still wanted him. Therefore; I developed this lust for the man who only had eyes for my sister.

"Did you two ever touch inappropriately?"

"Never Yariah. We've never engaged in nasty talking, texting, flirting or anything. When I say it was simply a crush, that's all it was."

"Why were you sending him nasty videos?" I rolled my eyes at the thought of Lori's lies.

"Sis, I did send him a few messages asking if he'd ever consider messing with me and his answer flat out was no. I tried flirting with him and he never took the bait."

"That's not what Lori said."

"I know and it's the exact reason I beat her ass." I moved to where she was and held her hand in mine.

"Riah, I was wrong for tryna push up on him and I'm really sorry, but she added all that extra stuff to hurt you. Haven't you learned by now she hates you for the exact reason Tasheem did?"

"It's not my fault Caleek doesn't want them." I smiled at her innocence.

"Yes it is. Don't you know you're forcing him, and he doesn't want you?" She started laughing.

"I'm really sorry Yariah and I don't know why I was so angry with you when my anger had nothing to do with you."

"Ro, you're my sister and I'm gonna love you regardless but don't ever allow a man to come in between us. You had me believing you hated me for reasons I had no clue of."

"I know." I put my head down.

"Now that we've moved on from that. Tell me about Bongi." She sat Indian style on the bed and started smiling. They all knew we were seeing each other but we've never talked because we weren't on speaking terms like that.

"I don't know now because Lori shouted all that out."

"Why would your best friend do that?" She put up air quotes.

"Because no matter how many times y'all got into it, I always had your back and she hated it. She felt as if I was supposed to put her first and agree with all the shit she was doing."

"See that's why I don't have friends. Bitches ain't shit." We started laughing.

"I'm serious. Amara is the only friend I have, and I know she won't do stupid shit to me because of Cazi." She spoke highly of Amara.

"Yea. We all know he don't play about Riah." I think Cazi felt bad and protected her more because the two of us were out the house and my mom was doing dumb shit.

"Honestly Ro, Amara is an amazing person and her heart is very pure. You have no idea the amount of hurt and pain she suffered when Cazi cheated on her. Shit, I wanted to beat his ass for her."

"But an abortion? When the hell did she get one?"

"I don't know Ro. I can't even tell you I knew about it because I found out when everyone else did."

"You think it was Cazi baby?"

"Daddy asked me the same thing and to be honest I don't know. Remember she disappeared for those months and only called here and there. I have no idea where she was or if it were another man."

"Did you see Cazi face?" I asked.

"Yea. That's why I told Leek to go back there with him."

"I don't think he'd hurt her but then again; he was really mad." I said, and she agreed.

"What you gonna do about Bongi?" She changed the subject.

"I'm hoping when Caleek speaks to him he'll at least talk to me." I glanced down at my phone and opened the messages. He opened each one I sent and left me on read. At least he knows how I feel.

"You love him?"

"Yea but I'm not sure it's gonna work. I mean I definitely wanna be with him but it's something about his baby mama that's rubbing me the wrong way."

"What you mean, and I didn't know he had kids."

"Two. A girl and a boy."

"Wow!" She was as shocked as me when I found out.

"Sis, I met them two weeks ago and they are the most adorable kids I've ever seen. His daughter clung to me get second we met, and his son kept tryna kiss me." I smiled thinking about meeting them.

"Aww I can't wait to meet them."

"Sis I'm not sure we're gonna last. His baby mama is on some other shit."

"It ain't no problem to beat her ass." She laughed and picked up her phone.

"Hey babe." I loved to see how happy she was.

"Ok. Be careful and don't get in trouble. I don't wanna have to come down to the station and fight big Bertha again." After she hung up, she started telling me about her small arrest. I say small because no one is gonna let her go to jail for Tasheem's bullshit.

"You won't be fighting with my niece or nephew inside." Her mouth dropped.

"You forgot I was at the hospital too?" I questioned due to her response.

"I guess." She rubbed her stomach.

"What did he say?"

"I was going to tell him but you knocked on the door."

"Well you better tell him soon because you'll be showing. And it's no telling how Tasheem will react." She waved me off.

"You know it's gonna be some shit because she's not going to let you take him."

"At this point I don't even care Ro. I have to protect this baby and pray Caleek and Cazi keep me safe." I noticed her getting teary eyed.

"I don't know what I would do if someone kidnapped me." I hugged her.

"It's not gonna happen." I said consoling her.

"Thank goodness you two made up." My father busted in the room. I think he was happier than we were.

"What are you two ladies about to do?" He asked and wrapped his arm around us.

"Nothing." I answered.

"Let's go celebrate me having my first grand baby."

"Daddy I ate." Riah whined and we looked at the plates on her dresser.

"It's still food there which means my grand baby hungry." We both laughed and walked out with him. I'm happy my sister and I were speaking too. It's been a long time and I missed her.

# *Tasheem*

"Tasheem, Caleek is here." My mom yelled through the bathroom door. I guess he wasn't lying about picking me up for breakfast.

"Ok. Let him know I'll be down shortly." I finished in the shower and hurried to put my clothes on. I was happy Tone got outta here early. I didn't want Caleek to see him. It doesn't matter he went to Yariah, I'm still gonna try my best to win him back.

I looked in the mirror and checked myself over to make sure no hickeys were left. Tone is a smart ass and I wouldn't put anything past him.

Once I realized nothing was there, I grabbed my things, closed my bedroom door and walked downstairs. I bit down on my lip staring at Leek. He was so got damn sexy to me and I had a quick flashback of how he used to handle my body.

"Hey." I spoke first.

"What up? You ready?" He had his head in the phone.

"Yea."

"A'ight let's bounce." He lifted his head and smiled.

"You look nice." Now it was my turn to smile. I had on some fitted jeans, a fitted shirt showing off my cleavage and a pair of ankle boots. I thought my outfit was cute but it's nice to know he noticed.

He opened the door and followed behind me. My mouth dropped staring at the Phantom sitting in front of the house. He had me in a truck when we left the hospital, so this is different. I wonder if the bitch knows he picking me up in this? Not that I care but it's always nice to piss her off.

"What you want to eat?" He asked when he sat on the driver's side. I shrugged my shoulders.

"Honestly, I'm not hungry so it's whatever you want."

"Well it's after eleven now. We can do lunch if you want." I told him and put my seatbelt on as he drove off.

He pulled up at the diner we used to frequent at a lot. They had the best burgers and he knew how much I enjoyed this place. I've never been the chick who had to eat at expensive spots. I looked over and smiled because I had no idea he remembered. It's the little things that made me smile with him.

When we stepped out the car, I tried holding his hand and he pulled it back. I don't know why. His fake ass girlfriend ain't here and even she were, he's still my man. I understand why he moved on but like I told my mother, we never broke up. He's still my fiancé and we need to focus on that. No I'm not delirious or losing my mind either. It's the truth.

"Will it be just you two?" The hostess asked at the door.

"Yes and can we have a booth in the corner?" He asked, and I turned to look at him.

"What? I expect you to explain everything and no one needs to hear." I admit my heart sank hearing him say that. I thought he wanted a corner spot to be alone. We'll be alone but not in the way I want. We started following the lady.

"Why the fuck did you bring me here if this bitch was here?"

"Who you talking about?" He glanced around the diner and smiled when his eyes laid on her. She was sitting there laughing with her sister and father. I wanted to know what the fuck is so funny when she's about to do time?

"You got one more time to call my girl a bitch."

"Really?"

"Really? Follow her to the booth and I'll be right there." I rolled my eyes and watched him stroll over to them.

"Here you go? Melissa will be your waitress. Enjoy." The hostess handed me the menu's and walked away. I couldn't even focus on shit and slammed the menu down. I stormed over to where they were and stopped in front of the table.

"Hello Tasheem. It's good to see you're ok." Their father said, and I gave him a fake smile. I'm not even mad at him but then again, I hate anyone who's ok with them being together.

"Caleek why are you over here with the woman who abducted me? And how the fuck are you even out? Did you bail her out?"

"Tasheem go the fuck on." Leek spoke through gritted teeth. He hated for people to cause a scene in public.

"Have fun now bitch because I promise when my lawyers get done with you, the only way you'll see him is through a fucking glass."

"Tasheem." She said my name and stood. Caleek got in between.

"I understand you're running off emotions."

"What?" I had my arms folded.

"You just came back and found out Caleek is with someone else and you're unhappy. You wanna pick up where you left off but I'm here to tell you, if it's a fight you want, I'll give it to you. However; my man won't allow me to put hands on you and neither will this bogus ass lawsuit and allegation you have against me. Trust that our time will come, and you better hope I take it easy on you."

"Is that a threat?" I asked and started taking off my earrings.

"Nope! It's a fucking promise bitch."

"Bitch." I reached over and smacked the fuck outta her.

"YOOOO! The fuck you doing?" Caleek pushed me into a table and I hit my head on the edge. My body hit the ground hard as hell. Outta nowhere, punches were being thrown all over my face. I tried to hit back but whoever it was kept them coming fast.

"That's enough Aphrodite." I heard and saw outta the eye that wasn't closed, her father lifting her off me.

"FUCK THAT DADDY! WHO THE FUCK SHE THINK SHE IS?" She screamed. Someone helped me off the floor and if Caleek could kill me with his eyes, I'd be six feet under for real.

"Go get your shit." He wasn't yelling and that scared me the most.

"Caleek its fine. Ro got her." Riah had his hand in hers as she tried calming him down.

"Its not ok Riah. Look at your got damn face." I smirked at the redness on it. At least, I got a hit off. I picked my things up and went to where he stood.

"I'm ready."

"Bounce bitch." He said and walked out with Yariah and her family. The manager came over and asked them to leave in the middle of it all.

"Caleek you brought me here."

"And you showed your ass. Since you tough, take your tough ass out my face and find a ride home." He sat Yariah in the front seat of the car I just came out of.

"Caleek."

"GET THE FUCK OUT MY FACE BEFORE I REALLY FUCK YOU UP." He was in my face with his fist balled up.

"We were supposed to talk." I whined.

"WHAT PART OF GET THE FUCK OUT MY FACE DON'T YOU GET?"

"Caleek lets go." Yariah had gotten out the car and grabbed his hand. As she pushed him away, I took my chance to get her the way I wanted. I yanked her hair and started raining blows on her face. Her sister started hitting me, but I didn't care because I had this bitch hair and swinging her all over. I was fucking her up too.

*CLICK!* I felt the cold steel on my temple.

"Let my girl's fucking hair go." I released it and put my hands up.

"I have never in my life wanted to beat a bitch's ass the way I wanna do you right now." He still had the gun on my temple.

"If you ever put your fucking hands on her again, I'll kill you and I put that on all my future kids." He pushed me away and I fell flat on my face.

"CALEEK!" I shouted.

"Fuck you bitch. I hope whoever kidnapped you, comes back and kills you next time."

"CALEEK!" Yariah yelled.

"Nah fuck that. I brought her here to talk about what happen and help her find out who did this so we can make sure they don't ever fuck with her again. Then she pulls this bullshit." He put his gun in the back of his waist and walked towards me.

"Caleek please. Let's just go." Yariah was now crying.

"Beat her ass Caleek. Look at my sisters face." He yoked me up by my shirt.

"Now go back to that nigga you fucked last night." I didn't say anything.

"Yea, you thought I didn't know the nigga stayed the night." He chuckled but not in a good way.

"Popping all that shit and you probably fucked him." He gave me a disgusting look.

"I had someone watching your house to make sure you were safe because even though I'm with her, I didn't want anything to happen to you. But guess what?" I wanted to speak but he had me at a loss for words. I should've known someone was watching the house.

"Let that nigga help you out. I'm done." He released my shirt and I fell back on the ground.

"As far as this bullshit ass charge you're tryna pin on Yariah; trust me she won't do a day in jail. We both know she's not responsible." He started walking away.

"CALEEK YOU'RE MY FIANCE. WE NEVER BROKE UP. HOW COULD YOU LEAVE ME?" I was now crying. He stopped and turned around.

"The minute you died, we were no longer together." I sat there looking stupid as hell. What could I say? I was caught and nothing I said would change the outcome of what transpired here today.

I picked my things up off the ground and went back in the diner. The manager offered me ice and paper towels. I took them and asked for her to contact the police. This bitch is going to jail for something.

****************************

"What happened to you?" My mother asked the second my feet crossed the threshold of her door.

"Nothing."

"That don't look like nothing." Luther said and strolled out the kitchen eating a sandwich.

"I finally beat up that bitch Riah."

"Tasheem NO!" My mom cried out and covered her mouth.

"You sure you beat her up because from the looks of things, I'd say she dragged yo ass." Luther started laughing after saying it.

"No, I did but her sister jumped on me from behind."

"WHAT?" Luther shouted. I started explaining what took place after Caleek and I left the house. All my mother did was shake her head in disgust. She told me to leave Yariah alone, but I couldn't do it. All these years of flirting with Caleek, talking slick to me and kidnapping me made me snap.

For those assuming I'm setting Yariah up and tryna frame her, why would I? What am I getting out of it? I lost damn near two years of my life, lost my child and fiancé. I know she did it and I'm gonna make sure she pays. Caleek better get his time in now because the lawyer I have, has never lost a case. She loved putting thugs away as she calls them and in her eyes that's exactly what Yariah is.

We've come to the conclusion the bitch hired people to set up the ambush with Caleek and I, shoot me and make the warehouse explode. The only thing is, I can't for the life of me remember anything. I recall someone shooting and another person falling on top of me, then I remember waking up three weeks ago in a hospital outside Virginia.

Don't ask how I got there or why I don't recall the last two years, but I don't. I've tried and even the doctors said my blood was full of so much drugs it's possible my memory is erased, or I suffered amnesia all that time.

He said the person(s) who held me against my will, knew what they were doing. I may or may not ever know what happened but to keep an open mind that some things will be familiar. I don't know how that'll work when I have no idea where I was even held. All I can do is hope for the best and pray I remember something.

"I told you to leave him alone. Tasheem why are you even bothering him when that man stayed here last night?" My mom had my face in her hands as she spoke.

"What man? Don't say Tone?" Luther spit as he talked. He was messy as fuck when he ate.

"Yup. It was him." My mother answered for me.

"Sis you need to stay away from him." He came towards me.

"I thought you were cool with him." I walked in the kitchen to get some ice for my eye.

"I was in the beginning; especially since I couldn't stand Caleek."

"Boy shut up. How are you mad with him when you were the one stealing?" My mom popped him on the back of the head after shouting out why Caleek hated him.

"He could've given me another job tho. I'm just saying." Luther was dead ass serious. I laughed at his ignorance.

"Why don't you like Tone?" I cracked the ice tray, put some in a paper towel and placed it on my eye. My mother went upstairs to lay down.

"When you supposedly died, he was hurt and was here almost everyday. Months went by and he stopped dropping by a lot which is fine but when I called and told him you were alive, he screamed on the phone and I quote, *How the fuck did that happen?*"

"Hmmm. It doesn't seem weird. I'd probably ask the same thing if he was supposed to be dead in an explosion." I told him.

"Maybe but if I were you, I'd watch him." He took his two fingers and went back and forth from my eyes to his.

"You crazy."

"I'm serious. Tasheem." He came closer to me.

"I fucked up with Caleek, but he really loved you." I rolled my eyes.

"Regardless of who he's with now, he broke down at the funeral. That man was distraught, and I didn't make it no better by telling him you were pregnant by Tone."

"WHAT?"

"I was mad sis. I blamed him for you dying."

"Luther."

"Don't worry. He beat my ass for saying it." I shook my head listening to him tell me more about my fake funeral. If Caleek was so upset, then why doesn't it seem that way? Whatever the case, I'm still taking that bitch down.

# *Caleek*

"Put the ice on your face Riah." I had to force her to do it because all she wanted to do is sleep. I was so got damn mad at Tasheem, I never got the chance to find out what happened and at this point I don't even care.

What's crazy is I wanted to help my ex, which is why I made it my business to take her out to breakfast. I knew Riah had nothing to do with her disappearance and so did everyone else. The hatred Tasheem had towards my girl is the only reason why she made the accusation. If she took the time out to think for a minute, she'd know someone close to her had to do this. It's the only thing I could come up with because when the attack took place, I wasn't beefing with anyone. It's not to say she had any with someone either but it's definitely a coincidence.

Then we get to the diner and Tasheem's stupid ass gets in her feelings and verbally and physically attacks Yariah. I'm happy Ro beat her ass though because I almost knocked Tasheem the fuck out. How the hell is she mad at a woman I chose? Of course we flirted a lot but we never crossed the line until she passed. Granted, the whole scenario would've gone different because like I told Yariah, I never would've made it down the aisle. My feelings were too strong for me to be unhappy with someone else.

"I need to go to the hospital." I snapped my neck to look at her. She was bent over and holding her stomach.

"What's wrong?" I rushed to where she stood and grabbed her hand.

"I didn't want you to find out this way but I'm pregnant." A smile graced my face but so did worry.

"Let's go." I carried her to the car and raced to the hospital.

On the way over I thought about the change in her body I never paid attention to. When we first had sex, she was wild and handled me like a pro. The second time she still could but as of lately she would stop me and mention certain positions hurting. Then she's been sleeping and crying a lot. The signs were there, and I ignored them. How stupid could I be? A nigga was happy as fuck but then again worried because this bitch fought her and what of she lost it?

I parked in the ER, helped her out and inside. The receptionist took her information, so I ran out to park. When I came back in, they were placing her in a wheelchair and said she needed to go upstairs.

On the way, I text Cazi and told him we were there. It's only been 24 hours and shit is all fucked up. We still don't know who aimed for Riah and ended up almost killing Amara. I've been tryna find Lori because I needed to know what's up with her and the baby. The bitch won't answer any calls or text messages. Last but not least, I see Tasheem is going to be a fucking problem.

One of the cops at the precinct sent me a text saying Tasheem called them to the diner. I told him to pull the tapes and see why the fight took place. She tried to say Yariah started it. I think she forgot in this day and age, the world is full of cameras. I hate to say it but I can already tell it's gonna be me to kill her.

I'm not saying she deserves to die but Tasheem is well aware that when I make a threat, or should I say promise, I always follow through. I understand why she'd think we were still a couple but like I told her, how you claiming us as one and the same nigga you were supposedly pregnant by stayed the night. She most likely fucked him, and I don't even care. I literally stopped by to find out what happened and look; a nigga still don't know. Oh well, he can help her figure it out.

"You can change into this gown and lay on the bed." The nurse told Riah. I closed the door and helped her get undressed.

"Caleek, I don't wanna go through this drama the entire pregnancy."

"You won't."

"My face tho." She pointed to it and it was fucked up. At first, I couldn't understand why Yariah wasn't hitting Tasheem back but after finding out she's pregnant, I see why.

She got some good hits on Riah, but it didn't take away from how pretty she was. There was a gash above her eye and her face was swollen. Tasheem may have pulled some of her hair out because she had a grip on it. Otherwise; she was still the same woman I fell in love with. Ro definitely beat the shit outta her in the restaurant and again outside. That reminds me, I still had to speak with Bongi.

"This don't mean shit." I pushed her hair back and kissed her.

"I'm gonna beat her ass when I deliver."

"No you won't."

"Yes I am. Fuck that." She climbed in the bed.

"She'll be handled before then." Riah stopped pulling the sheets over her legs and stared at me.

"Leek, I don't want you doing anything you may regret." I finished pulling the sheets up and sat next to her.

"The only thing I regret is missing out on so much time with you." She smiled and ran her hand down my face.

"Ok let's see what's going on." The doctor shouted as he walked in jolly as hell. The nurse came in pushing a machine. He had Riah lay back, placed the gel on her stomach and showed us the screen.

"Here's your baby." Riah grabbed my hand.

"Damn you're giving me a baby." I leaned down to kiss her and asked the doctor to print me out a photo. He wanted her to stay for another hour to monitor the baby and then we could leave. He also had to give her four butterfly stitches above her eye and told her she could only take Tylenol for headaches.

"How are you gonna handle two kids at once?" Riah questioned when the doctor and nurse stepped out.

"First off, I don't know if that's my kid with Lori and if it is, we'll be taking care of two babies." She laughed but I'm serious.

"You must be outta yo mind if you think I can handle two kids on my own." I told her and meant every word.

"Awwww. I'll help you baby." We sat there discussing the kids, the new house and anything else we could before the doctor discharged her.

After getting her home and situated, I drove to the bar. I needed to get this crap done too so I could it be over with. I didn't wanna hear my girls' mouth.

********************

"What up yo?" I grabbed a pool stick and watched Bongi set up a new rack.

"Shit. What's going on?"

"Man, I can't even tell you." I was being honest. It was so much going on, I couldn't tell anyone shit because some I didn't know.

"What you mean?" He asked picking up the other stick.

"Besides my ex fiancé, or as she says, my fiancé returning from the dead, my girl told me I had to talk to you about Ro." I bent down and hit the first ball splitting the rack.

"I'm good."

"You tryna convince me or yourself?" I missed the hole by an inch.

"I said I'm good." He responded with an attitude.

"You're good huh?" I walked over to him.

"Aren't you the same nigga who told me Aphrodite was the best you ever had? I clearly remember you saying she may be the one." I rested my chin on top of the pool stick and waited for him to answer.

"Yea well. That was before I found out she was crushing on my boy." He moved over for me to take my turn.

"Look Bongi. You know I've never been one to sugar coat shit." He looked at me.

"Would I feel some kind of way learning the chick I'm falling for had a crush on my boy? HELL YEA!" He gave me the *ok then* look.

"But I'd ask her questions instead of jumping to conclusions."

"Leek man. I do not wanna hear how she wants you. And then she sent you freaky videos and shit. Bro she was doing that for me." I started laughing.

"She never sent me any videos, nor did she send me nasty messages." He stopped and stared at me.

"She did mention her crush to me a few times and asked if I'd ever fuck with her like that and I flat out told her no."

"What you tryna say? My girl ain't ugly." He caught himself and both of us busted out laughing.

"Lori was saying any and everything to get under Yariah's skin. She knew mentioning that would hurt my girl and it did." I stood next to him.

"Bro, if at any chance something went down between us I considered inappropriate or thought you should know, I would've told you."

"Leek I don't know."

"She wasn't on no stalker shit and like I said nothing ever happened between me and your girl." He waved me off.

"Now after I beat your ass in this game I'ma need you to call or go see her. She getting on my damn nerves about talking to you."

"What?" He asked in an uncertain tone.

"She ain't calling me nigga. She asked her sister in a text and on the phone if I spoke to you yet." I saw a grin creep on his face.

"She's really into you and Riah said she thinks Ro is in love with you." He lifted his beer and took a sip.

"Why are you tryna get me to call her?"

"Like I said, my girl was getting on my nerves and after she beat the brakes of Tasheem for Riah, I felt like I owed her anyway."

"I told her not to be fighting."

"Nah, I can't front. Tasheem snuck my girl twice and after finding out Riah pregnant and couldn't do anything, Ro did exactly what she was supposed to."

"Oh shit. I didn't know all that happened. Where she at?" He questioned, and I shrugged my shoulders.

"I'll call her in a few days." He had a sneaky ass grin on his face.

"Nigga really?"

"Hell yea really. You know how good that make up sex about to be." I almost fell from laughing so hard. At least, I know he's over the other shit. Now all I have to do is figure out what really happened to Tasheem and handle that. If she's back, either she had to be in on the abduction or someone made a mistake and let her go.

Bongi and I ended up staying there until closing. The two of us were fucked up. He refused to call Ro to pick him up, so we called Mark. He pulled up going off because we didn't invite him. Drunk and all, I felt a presence watching as I got in the car.

"I seen him too." Mark said without me saying a word.

"Seen who?" Bongi was worse off than me.

"Tone." Is all I said and laid my head on the seat. He's gonna be a motherfucking problem.

## *Amara*

"Cazi." I whispered and glanced around the room. Monitors were beeping, and it was dark. The TV was on but besides that you couldn't see.

"AHHHHHH!" I screamed out when I tried to move.

"YO! WHY THE FUCK MY WIFE SCREAMING LIKE THAT?" I heard and directed my eyes to the door. Cazi came in wearing a scowl on his face and his father behind him. He flicked the light on and I smiled and how handsome he was.

"Are you ok Mrs. Perry?" The nurse rushed to my side.

"My lower half is in extreme pain and why can't I move?"

"Mrs. Perry you were in an accident and..."

"Get yo stupid ass outta here. I'll fucking tell her." Cazi barked and the nurse damn near ran out the room.

"How are you sweetie?" His father spoke and moved closer.

"I'm hurting. How long have I been here?" I asked him and couldn't help but notice my husband being very distant. His body was leaned against the wall and he barely looked at me.

"You've been here three days so far." His father was the only one answering me.

"Three days?" I questioned because it didn't feel that long.

"You were in and outta consciousness and the doctor said it was the medication." I listened to his father tell me they were all ecstatic I made it and wishing me a speedy recovery.

"Cazi what's wrong? Is Yariah ok?" He lifted his head.

"Pops can you give us a minute?"

"I don't think that's a good idea." I was shocked his father said that.

"What's going on?" I let out another yell as I tried to move my body in a seated position.

"Stop moving yo." Cazi barked and closed the door when his father left.

"Baby what's wrong?" He came closer, ran his hand down my face and stared.

"Why did you wanna get married so quick Amara?" He sat down slowly next to me.

"What do you mean? We've been discussing marriage over the last year."

"You're right but I hadn't even proposed yet. You skipped the engagement part and dove head into a marriage. Why?" I thought about what he said. Cazi never proposed but we spoke so much on marriage and he really showed and proved he wasn't cheating, I figured why not? Then again, I'd thought he'd leave me when he found out my truth.

"Cazi what's this about?"

"I think you know. But since you need to hear it; let me." He gave me a slight smile. I just let the tears fall when he said began talking.

"The doctor informed me your pelvis is fractured, your nose is broke and so is your leg. It's going to be a long healing process." I nodded.

"Oh! I almost forgot. They had a hard time tryna stop the internal bleeding due to the massive amount of scar tissue inside." If my body could stiffen up, I'm sure it did.

"Cazi let me explain."

"Explain what Amara? How you knew it would be very hard for you to get pregnant due to some fucking abortion you had and tried to keep a secret?" I saw the anger brewing.

"Cazi it wasn't like that."

"Oh no because my girl having trouble conceiving and didn't think she should tell me is a problem."

"I wanted to tell you. I didn't know how."

"Tha fuck you mean you didn't know how?" He stood and started pacing.

"You and I just got back together, and I didn't wanna lose you again."

"Sooooo you allow all this time to pass and not once did it cross your mind to tell me? Here I'm thinking something's wrong with me and it's been you the entire time." I sat there watching his temper grow.

"Is that what the doctor meant when he said, after what she's been through it's gonna take a while?" I put my head down

"I want the truth to this next question." I wiped my eyes and looked at him.

"Is it the reason you rushed to get married? You knew once I found out it would be a wrap?"

"Regardless, of why I married you sooner than later, I still wanted to be your wife."

"IS IT?" He shouted and made me nervous.

"Yes."

"What the fuck Amara?"

"Cazi, I wanna carry your kids and grow old with you. Nothing has changed." He chuckled.

"Nothing has changed huh? If I took you home and made love to you, are you going to get pregnant?" I didn't say anything.

"I fucked up Amara, but you should've told me.

"I'm sorry Cazi and you're right."

"Was the baby mine?" I gave him a crazy look.

"Cazi." I didn't wanna answer the question.

"Amara it happened during the months we weren't together, so I wish the fuck you would keep quiet. Now like I said, was the child mine?"

"No.

*CRASH!* The tray table was flipped upside down. He threw the chair at the window and it cracked. Those windows are strong as hell. It only let me know he used all his strength to toss it. I wanted to go over to him but my body was in so much pain from the accident, it wasn't anything I could do to stop him. The door busted open and his father, Caleek and my parents rushed in.

"What's going on?" My mother asked.

"Nothing. Please just give us a minute." I cried and begged for them to leave.

"Amara." Caleek tried to talk me out of it.

"Please just go." I watched each of them step out and waited for Cazi to relax. His breathing was erratic, and I wasn't even sure he calmed down because he was facing the window with his back turned. I started telling him what happened anyway.

"Cazi the night or should I say the day I found you in the hotel room, I was devastated. I couldn't understand for the life of me what I did wrong or why you cheated. I was the perfect girlfriend to you, cooked, cleaned, fucked you whenever and wherever you wanted. There wasn't anything I wouldn't do for you and in one night you destroyed everything we built for a piece of pussy." He stood there in silence.

"My heart was broken; my mind was all over the place and you have no idea how many times I contemplated killing myself." He swung his body around.

"I stayed in a hotel room under my parents name which is why you couldn't find me. I cut myself off from the world just so I wouldn't hear anyone ask *if I were ok, did I need anything* or all the other questions they ask when someone's been hurt." I used the sheet to wipe my eyes and the snot running out my nose. That too was a task in itself due to the nose brace.

"I had bottles of pills, a rope, a big hunter's knife and a gun because I couldn't decide how I wanted to end my life. Shit, I even wrote the suicide letter." I shook my head at the thought.

"Day after day I sat in the room going over the reasons in my head on why you did it, why I wasn't good enough and to this day I still don't know." He moved closer and I asked him not to touch me. I didn't need his sympathy.

"One night I went out on my own, met some guy in the bar, got drunk and had a one-night stand." He sucked his teeth.

"All I wanted was for you to find me and go through the same emotions I did when I found you in that room? I even sent you a message to the other room me and the guy went to. Unfortunately, you never came and what I did was in vain. I hurt myself because I've always told you the thought of laying with another man made me sick and the entire time, he and I shared a bed I had to stop myself from crying. He wasn't you and I retreated to doing the exact same thing you did to me. We weren't together but still. I have never been a woman to seek revenge, but you pushed me."

"Damn." He whispered and put his head down.

"You and I were on speaking terms a month after and two days later I learned of the pregnancy. I loved you so much and was happy to even be speaking to you I never mentioned it. I felt since you never came it's something I'd never talk about, and I couldn't risk losing you again. No matter how bad I wanted you to hurt, I couldn't do it."

"FUCKKKKKKK!" I shouted when I tried to move again.

"Amara." He reached out for me.

"Don't touch me Cazi." I smacked his hand away.

"The day of the abortion you and Caleek went outta town on business for a week. After the procedure everything was fine. Two or three days later the bleeding got so bad I could barely move. My mom came over and took me to the hospital. Sad to say the person who performed the abortion was a fake doctor and practicing illegally." I laid my head back on the pillow. I noticed a tear sliding down his cheek.

"I didn't have the kind of money you have Cazi and I had to go where my insurance paid. Regardless of it being a fake practice, he took my HMO."

My insurance company didn't even know it was a bad place. I have a lawsuit against them too because as much money I pay to them, they should've never sent me there. My lawyer said its their responsibility to make sure the doctors' offices are legit. I didn't tell Cazi about the lawsuit because then he'd ask questions. Even though I'm telling him now, I still don't need to mention it.

"Long story short, he messed me up and I almost died. I can have babies Cazi. It's just going to take me longer." I turned my head.

"You have no idea how much I regret doing it. I'm sorry for not telling you and yes, it's the exact reason I wanted to marry you quickly. I knew you'd be upset and most likely would leave me." He remained silent and I couldn't read his demeanor.

"If you want to get this marriage annulled go ahead, since you feel like it was under false pretenses. I don't need your money and I won't ask for anything. You can have it all. I won't fight it." I turned to look at him.

"All I ask is you help pay for my medical care if my insurance company denies me. I don't wanna be stuck in a wheelchair forever." He let his head fall back for a few minutes, stood, kissed my forehead and walked out without saying a word.

"Are you ok honey?" My mom came running in.

"I told him." Her and my father looked at me. She hugged me and said it would be alright, but would it be?

************************

"It's hurting." I told the nurse and physical therapist. It's been a week and half since the accident, and they were tryna help me stand.

I fractured my pelvis and the doctor said since it wasn't a bad one, I needed to try and stand with crutches. You can't cast a pelvis, and it has to basically heal on its own. He didn't want me to put weight on my body, but he also didn't want me lying in bed all day either.

I'm not sure what he expected with a broken leg too. I mean it was only from the knee down, but it's still broken. The pain is unbearable at times, yet I'm determined to fight through it and walk again.

The doctor specifically informed the insurance company I had to stay for at least six weeks, and they didn't have an issue with it. I'm actually at a rehabilitation place getting all the help I need. It's a very nice spot too.

I hadn't seen nor heard from Cazi and shockingly I'm ok. I was preparing myself for the annulment papers anyway now. I removed the wedding ring from my finger and had my mother go retrieve as much as she could from his house while he was at work.

I asked her not to take too much because he'll notice, and I don't want or need anything he purchased. I really only asked for personal papers, my laptop, and anything else she'd think I'd considered important.

"You only have to stand on your good leg for a minute or two." The therapist told me. I blew my breath and stood. Whether the doctor considered it a bad fracture or not, the shit still hurt like hell.

"Look at you." Yariah walked in smiling. I really loved her. She's been by my side since I woke up.

"I'm trying."

"You'll be walking soon." She put her purse on the chair and walked over to me.

"I hope so because I'm tired of laying in the bed." They all laughed and after a few minutes of standing, I asked to get back in the bed. The therapist and nurse assisted while Riah put the covers over my legs. It was chilly as hell in here even with the slipper socks.

"You're gonna be outta here before you know it." She sat in the bed next to me.

"I hope so. What's going on? I thought you weren't coming until tomorrow." I picked my cell up and checked my emails.

"I go to court in a couple of weeks to be arraigned or have my charges read to me. I was supposed to go a few days ago but the judge had an emergency and postponed it."

"Ok. I know you're not worried." I put my phone down.

"What if the judge believes her story? I don't wanna go to jail." She rested her head on my shoulder.

"Girl, you are not going to jail." I wiped her eyes.

"But..."

"But nothing. Your brother or Caleek won't allow it." She sat up and looked at me.

"Why did you do it?" I knew she was referencing the abortion because we haven't spoken of it.

"Long story short, I tried to hurt your brother the way he did me and failed. He never knew about me sleeping with another man until recently." I said all in one breath.

"I got the abortion because regardless if we were on break or not, I knew he'd never accept another child and I loved him. Shit, if he told me about another child, I wouldn't be able to accept it either." I shrugged my shoulders.

"Anyway, it was stupid of me to terminate my child and then I kept it a secret. I should've told him when we were on better terms. That's why I'm ok if he wants the marriage annulled."

"He's not gonna divorce you Amara."

"You didn't see his face sis. He was angry, sad and most of all disappointed and I don't blame him."

"You did what you felt was right at the time and it's in the past. Yes, you had every right to tell him, but he still loves you very much. He needs time to understand all of it."

"Well he can take all the time he needs because in my eyes I failed as a girlfriend if he cheated and failed as a wife because I can't even give him kids." I felt myself getting upset.

"If it was meant for y'all to have kids already it would've happened. Maybe this was God's way of making you tell him. Now that it's out in the open you can move forward."

"I don't know right now. The only thing I'm focused on is walking again. By the way, did they find the person yet?"

"No and I'm sorry this happened to you."

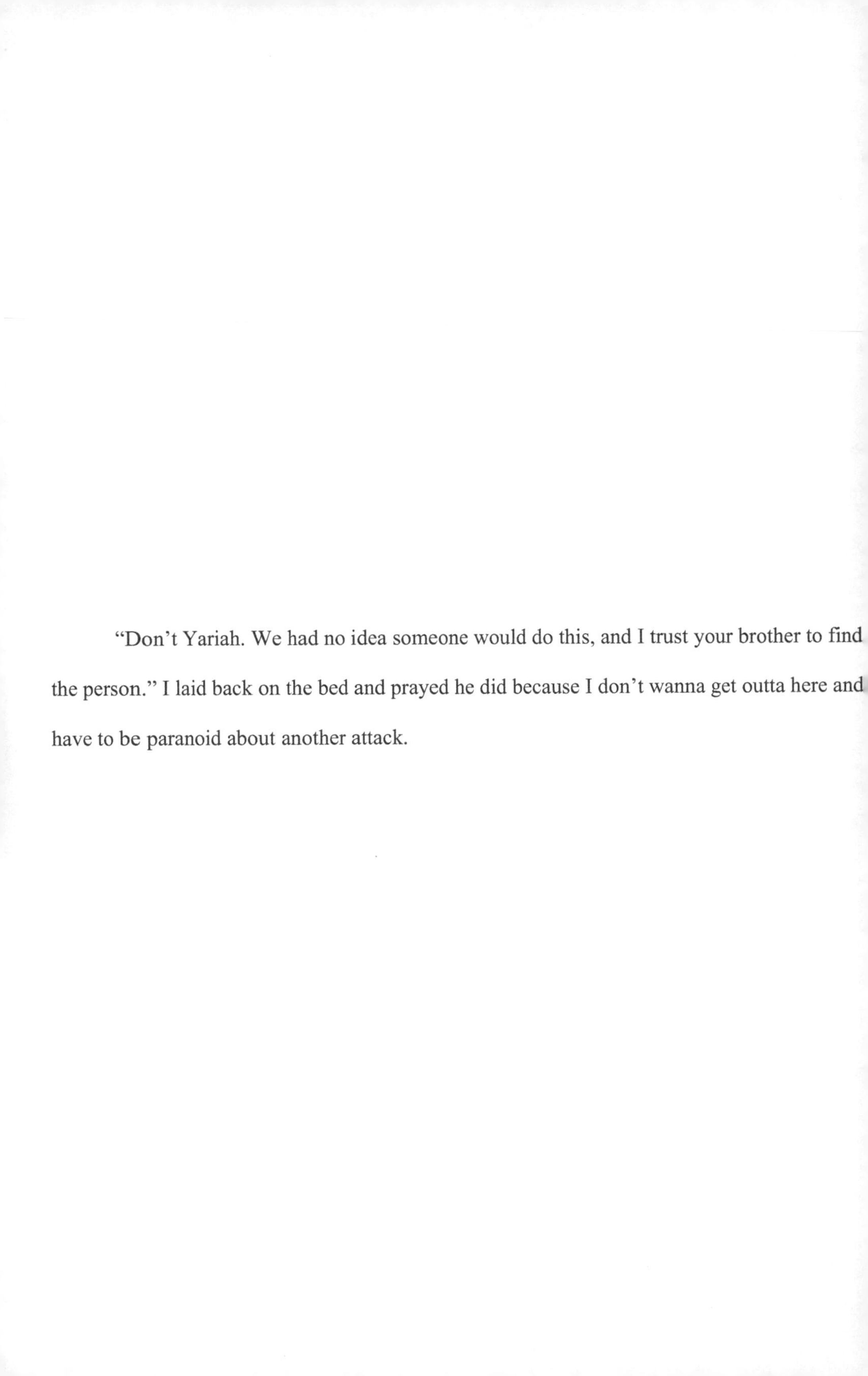

"Don't Yariah. We had no idea someone would do this, and I trust your brother to find the person." I laid back on the bed and prayed he did because I don't wanna get outta here and have to be paranoid about another attack.

# *Cazi*

"What happened to the money?" Caleek and I had the reverend hemmed up against the bookcase in his office.

"Please don't hurt me." He cried.

"This is my last time asking. Where…"

*BAM*

"Is…"

*BAM*

"The money?" Caleek split his eye open and the way his nose looked, you could tell it was fractured or broke.

"They took it." The reverend finally yelled out.

"They?" I questioned and pulled my boy off because he was about to kill him.

"Here." I handed him a few tissues to hold against his nose. Talking to him with blood everywhere looked disgusting.

"The day after Mr. Simms paid for the funeral, two people approached me on the way to the bank."

"Yea right." Caleek shouted from the other side of the room.

"They did. I filled out a police report and everything." He asked to be excused for a moment to use the bathroom. Since it's right in the room we had no problem letting him. When he came out his nose was still crooked, he had some paper towels against his eye and his face was swollen but at least it wasn't as much blood.

"The people told me the money was stolen and belonged to them. I didn't know what was going on and didn't care. I just wanted to stay alive."

"Then what happened?" Caleek questioned and stared at him with a blank expression.

"One of them said, now that we have his B." I started laughing because he wouldn't curse.

"We're gonna use her to get his money." Caleek and I looked at each other. The whole shit seems crazy because not once did we receive a ransom for Tasheem. There were a lot of unknown text messages, but nothing mentioned paying them.

"Did you see their faces?" I asked.

"Barely, but I can tell you one of them was a woman."

"Word?" Caleek responded. He was thinking the same as me. Whoever blew up the warehouse are the same ones who robbed him.

"Last question." Caleek walked up on him.

"Why didn't you tell me when it happened?"

"The guy said if I mentioned it to you, they'd kill my family. He said someone was watching me."

"Here's the money for the funeral. Anything Tasheem's parents paid, I want you to return." Caleek told him.

"But what if they follow me again?" You could tell how nervous he was.

"They can't get anything because this is a check. You're the only one who can cash it. As far as anyone following you, let me know if anything suspicious happens." Caleek said and stepped out the office. I gave the reverend both of our phone numbers and told him to call if there's any problems. It's obvious whoever did this is around the area.

"You know you're going to hell for beating the reverend up in church." I was cracking up walking to the truck.

"What the fuck ever. He should've told one of us. I thought he was tryna be slick and keep it."

"I did too but I would've at least pulled him outside the church." I kept cracking jokes on him

"You talking shit, but what's up with the stripper bitch?" My smile faded.

"Ain't shit funny now nigga." Now it was his turn to laugh.

"The results came in the mail." I told him and ran my hand over my head.

"Well? Do I have a nephew, niece or what?" I sat in the driver's side, pulled the console up and handed him the envelope.

"What's this?"

"I don't wanna open it." I was dead serious.

The results came in the mail the day after Amara was hit by the truck. It's one of the reasons I hadn't been up to the hospital to see her. Hell yea I was hurt hearing about the abortion and the real reason we had trouble conceiving, but I would've forgiven her, had she told me sooner.

I can be mad all I want listening to her describe in detail what she went through but it's my fault. Had I not cheated she would've never resulted in revenge. It's unfortunate we're going through a rough patch but it's what happens.

I almost snapped her got damn neck when she told me to get the marriage annulled. Tha fuck I look like allowing her to be with another man? Call me selfish all you want but if she ain't with me, she ain't with no one.

Now here I am watching my brother from another mother open the test results of a paternity test I never intended on taking. However; once the bitch showed up at my job it only made sense. My mother didn't make things better by announcing how much the child resembled me.

To be honest, one part wants to know, and the other doesn't. I mean how can I explain another child by a woman I had a one-night stand with? But then again, I want kids but only with my wife.

"In the case of..." Blah blah blah is all I heard coming from Caleek.

"BROOOOO!" He shouted and pointed in front of us. There was a kid standing there. I slammed on the breaks hard as hell.

"What the fuck?" Both of us hopped out the truck and ran over to him. He couldn't have been any older than six or seven.

"Why you out in the street like this?" Tears started racing down his face.

"Someone said if I didn't stand here, they'd kill my mom." Caleek and I both grabbed our weapon, the boy and jumped in the truck.

"Where you live?"

"Right there." He pointed down the street from where he stood.

"How many people in there?" I questioned. If we going in, it's best to know what we're dealing with.

"A lot. Please don't let them kill my mom. My little sister in there and she's just a baby."

"Let me get this right." I said rubbing my temples.

"Somebody told you to jump out in the road?"

"Yes, but they were waiting for this truck." Caleek and I looked at each other.

“They followed us from the church.” I said and we smiled because it’s exactly what we wanted. Unfortunately, this kid and his family were stuck in the middle.

“Go inside the store and don’t come out. Ask the owner to lock up and hide you.” I told him and stepped back out the truck.

“What about my mom and sister?” You could see his concern.

“We’re gonna try and get them out.” He nodded and ran in the store.

“How long?” I asked Leek who was on the phone with Bongi and the team.

“They’re six minutes away.”

“A’ight.” I pulled the truck over to stop blocking traffic and we both kept our eyes on the house. There were no cars in front of it and you couldn’t even tell anyone was home.

“What you think?” Leek asked and checked to make sure he had enough bullets. I reached under my seat and grabbed the box I had two handguns in and handed him one just in case.

“I think they want a war and whatever money you have.”

“Sheittttt they ain’t getting a fucking dime from me.” He said confidently. His phone started ringing.

“A’ight. Cazi and I going to the door. Soon as we kick it down, y’all come in.” He spoke to Bongi.

“You ready?”

“Yup.” We got out the truck, walked down the street like we belonged there and up on the porch. *Strike one*; with whoever this was, never let the opponent approach you. How you send a decoy outside and don’t attack? They should’ve come running out the minute I stopped the truck. *Fucking amateurs.*

"Yo, these some dumb motherfuckers." Leek whispered. Their cars were in the back and you could hear arguing inside. *Strike two*; never not pay attention because it can get you killed.

*BOOM!* I kicked the door hard as I could, and it fell off the hinges.

"OH SHIT!" Someone yelled out and shots were fired. The boy wasn't lying when he said it was a lot of them. Niggas were upstairs and some came from the basement. What type of shit they had going on over here?

"You good?" I asked Bongi who just busted in with more of the team.

"Yea. Where Caleek?" I turned and saw him with a gun to someone's head.

"Who that?"

"I don't know but he was shooting so I figured we'd ask questions before killing him." *Strike three*; Never, ever leave a team member behind.

"A'ight. Do what you need, and we'll check the rest of the house." Bongi and I slowly crept up the steps with others behind us. We went through each room, in the attic, back down the basement and in the backyard. In total there were about ten niggas, two chicks and a dog laid out.

"Damn shame what they did to the dog." Bongi said laughing.

"Yo! Where are all the pictures?" I asked because all women put photos up of their kids.

"They must've just moved in or were on their way out." Mark said and pointed to the many boxes spread out.

*POW! POW!* We heard and ran back in the house. Whoever dude was had his brains splattered on the wall. Caleek had a weird look on his face.

"What's up?"

"This nigga said the two people after us are from this area and we've seen them on more than one occasion. When I asked who they were, he refused to answer and said they'll show their face soon enough; especially if I killed him."

"So you killed him?" I asked.

"I had to. How else am I gonna get the motherfuckers to show their face?" Caleek shrugged and we all started laughing. That nigga may not show a lot of his ways but he's probably the worst outta all of us.

"Where's the chick and baby?" We all ran out the house just in time.

"We'll figure it out another time. We need to get the fuck outta here." Caleek yelled and all of us dispersed.

"We need to hurry up and find these motherfuckers. For him to say we know the people, don't sit right with me."

"Facts." I said. I dropped him off at home and went to my office. Whoever is behind this must not have realized they just fucked up.

# *Aphrodite*

"WHO IS IT?" I shouted from upstairs. Someone was ringing my doorbell and I damn sure wasn't expecting anyone.

"WHO IS IT?" No answer again. I really need to invest in one of those ring doorbells that show the person outside on your phone. I tossed the towel on the bed, threw my robe and slippers on and went down the steps to see who was here. I snatched the door open and was pushed back in.

"Don't ever open your door without being sure who's behind it." Bongi barked and closed the door with his foot.

"Umm, I didn't know you were coming over."

"Exactly! I could've been a killer and you opening the door with no care in the world." He yelled and plopped down on the couch. I haven't seen him in I don't know how long, and he come over talking shit. Who he think he is?

"I don't think anyone is looking to kill me but ok." I placed my hands on my hips.

"How can I help you?" I asked as he kicked his sneakers off.

"Is that blood?" I pointed to red shit under his shoe.

"FUCK!" He yelled and looked down at himself.

"I just got these Jordan's." I busted out laughing and went to grab a black garbage bag. I've been around long enough to know they have to be thrown away.

"Here." I turned around and he was standing there shirtless. I swallowed hard and tried to move past him.

"Where you going?" He put both hands on the wall to block me in.

"I was going to put your sneakers in a bag because..." He gripped my chin and made me look at him.

"Anymore secrets?" I shook my head no and when his lips touched mine that was it. The two of us went at it like dogs in heat. Make up sex is definitely the fucking best.

"Tell me everything." Bongi asked when we stepped out the shower. He dried me off and laid next to me in the bed. Here it is after three in the morning and he's asking me this dumb shit. The least he could've done is ask me tomorrow; I'm drained.

"It was only a crush and it's because he reminded me of my ex." I turned to face him.

"I was going through my own shit Bongi. I even took Caleek wanting her, out on my sister."

"Do you fantasize about him or wish he was here and not me?" I could hear the uncertainty in his voice, but he had nothing to worry about.

"HELL NO!" I pushed him on his back and climbed on top.

"You're the only man I want Bongi. I'm in love with you." He smirked and used his hands to grip my ass.

"I'm in love with you too." One of his hands slid through my hair. He brought my face closer to his.

"It's you and me Ro. I better not hear you entertaining another nigga or you and him gonna regret it."

"Well damn. Should I be worried?" I grinded my lower half on him.

"Very. I don't play when it comes to mine."

"Me either." He moved his arms under my legs and pulled me up on his face.

“We need to discuss your baby mama tho. Oh my gawdddddd.” His mouth latched on my clit and I couldn’t say anything else.

***********************

“Is Bongi here?” Tarshay asked with an attitude when I opened the door she was banging on. I tightened my robe up and placed my hand back on the doorknob. I’m pretty sure I’ll have to slam it in her face. How the hell does she know where I live anyway?

“Yea but he’s sleep.”

“Wake him up.” I didn’t like the way she was speaking to me. How you show up to someone’s house demanding shit?

*BOOM!* I slammed the door in her face. I know she’s aware he’s here because his car is sitting outside my house. Why not just ask to speak to him instead of beating around the bush with BS?

I walked away from the door, and stepped in the kitchen to make myself a cup of coffee. I had a great night and early morning. I’m not about to let his sour ass baby mama ruin my mood. I can’t even tell you why she is the way she is.

From the little Bongi told me about her, she works all the time, they split custody and barely speak unless it’s to go out or about the kids. He never discussed why they’re no longer together and I didn’t ask. I’ve learned that certain people will let you in on their personal lives when they’re ready in which he may not be.

I don’t care for her because the bitch got my phone number somehow after I met the kids for the first time. In the beginning, I was cool with it because if I’m gonna be around them she and I may as well get along. However, this bitch was on an entirely different level and I cursed her out and blocked her. She contacted me again from a different number and told me I better not have her kids calling me mommy, don't bathe them, don't do her daughters hair and the list goes on and on.

I hadn't mentioned it to Bongi because I can handle my own. Plus, he claims they're cool, and I don't wanna mess up any agreements they have with the kids. If it's meant for him to find out it'll happen.

*CRASH!* I dropped the cup out my hand and ran to my living room. Glass was everywhere from my bay window. I carefully walked over and saw a damn cinderblock on my floor. I ran out the door and started beating her ass.

"What the fuck happened?" Bongi came rushing down the steps in a pair of basketball shorts and no shirt. He pulled us apart and asked if I were ok.

"Ask her." I pointed to Tarshay picking herself up off the ground.

"This bitch wouldn't go get you when I came to the door." He focused back on me.

"Is that true Ro?" I shook my head and walked in my house. I didn't have time for his shit.

A few minutes later I heard a car pull off and my door slam. I ignored him and continued sweeping up the glass. He came behind and turned me towards him.

"What happened?"

"She knocked on the door demanding for me to wake you up. I slammed the door and she threw a fucking cinderblock through my window." I pointed to it on the ground. The shit was big as hell. How the hell did she even lift it?

"Bongi one thing I'm not gonna do is deal with baby mama drama. If that's how's it gonna be, you can bounce with her."

“This is why I didn’t wanna fall for you.” He pressed his lips on mine and ran up the steps. I dropped the broom and stormed up there. I leaned on the door frame as he began putting his clothes on.

“What you mean this is why...” He cut me off.

“The bitch is crazy.”

“I’d say.” He turned around.

“No, I’m serious. She’s fucking crazy.” He put more emphasis on the word crazy.

“Then why are you leaving?”

“Because if I don’t, she’ll do something to my kids.”

“WHAT?” He blew his breath and grabbed the Nike slippers he had from when he used to stay over.

“Anytime I find someone, she does any and everything to make them leave me alone.”

“Oh so you’ve been in love a bunch of times since her?” He smirked and walked up on me. I was a tad bit jealous when he said it.

“Nah, but you’re the first one I’m gonna fight for to stay in my life.”

“I’m lost.”

“Long story short, we’re cordial because of the kids. Whenever she thinks I’m serious with a woman she’ll do dumb shit like pinch my kids or take their toys. One time, she made Aleese stay in a dirty diaper for two days. By the time I got her, the rash was so bad child services got involved. They said it was neglect and gave me full custody.” He looked stressed as he finished talking.

"She went to parenting classes and passed with flying colors. The judge gave us joint custody again and I've been extra careful not to let her know who I'm with. Ro." He put my face in his hands.

"I don't know how she found out where you lived, and I'll pay for the window. All I ask is for you not to let her push you away. It's what she wants and expects."

"Bongi, I don't wanna be the reason she does bad things to your kids." He pressed his lips on mine and kissed me in a tender, yet passionate way.

"Nothing she does will be your fault Ro. I can't allow her to control my happiness." I smiled when he said it.

"You're happy with me?"

"Hell yea I am. I didn't come back for nothing." He smacked me on the ass and told me to call someone to fix the window and let them bill him.

"I'll call you in a few."

"Wait!" I ran down the steps.

"If she comes back, I'm beating her ass again?" He glanced around my place.

"I don't want you fighting, and I would never get mad at you for defending yourself."

"Just making sure." I folded my arms against my chest.

"Matter of fact don't stay here tonight. I don't know what she's up to. Call you in a few." He kissed me again and handed me the key off his ring. And just like that he was gone. I hope she doesn't do anything stupid.

## *Bongi*

"What the fuck is wrong with you?" I pushed Tarshay up against the wall at her mother's house. After Ro beat her ass, I made her get in the car and leave. I knew she'd come straight over because my kids are here and like I said, she would do fucked up shit to them if I didn't want her.

"What's going on Bongi?" Her mom came out the room with my daughter in her arms.

"Where's my son?" I took her and started to put the jacket on. My son was five and my daughter was three going on fifteen. She had a mouth on her and an attitude like her stinking ass mother.

Tarshay hasn't always been this way and hell no I'm not taking responsibility for her actions. I would never call my kids mother out her name, but this bitch is fucking crazy. It's the exact reason we can't be together now.

I didn't notice it in the beginning because like most niggas you try and do everything right at first. I gave her whatever she wanted, never cheated and gave her two kids. Nothing was good enough for her though. It sucks because you really do meet a motherfucker's representative before the actual person. They should come with a damn warning sign.

"Right here daddy. We leaving?" He came running in with his Nintendo switch.

"Yup. Where's your jacket?"

"You're not taking my kids." Tarshay had the nerve to say.

"I'm not in the mood."

"Me either." She picked her phone up.

"Yes 911. My kids' father is tryna kidnap my children." Her mom shook her head.

"What did she do?" I loved her mother because she never sugar coated anything her daughter did.

"I met someone and..."

"You did?" She smiled and told me it's about time. She loved me for her daughter but also said I needed to be with someone who appreciated me. Just like everyone else she knew her daughter was psycho.

"Your daughter shows up at her house and..." I looked to make sure my son wasn't coming and closed my daughters' ears.

"Threw a damn cinderblock through her window."

"Is that why your face looks like that?" Tarshay sucked her teeth.

"Yup and if I didn't break them up, I'm sure she would've looked worse."

"Go head son. I'll let the cops know what's going on." Before I could even step out the door, you could hear the sirens coming down the street. I don't know why she did it to herself. The officers got out as I started placing the kids in the car. I strapped my daughter in, and my son put the belt over his booster car seat.

"What up?" Mark asked laughing. Yup, he's on our team and a fucking cop. Why you think we get away with so much?

"She starting her shit again." I leaned against the car and watched as Tarshay told them the BS story about me taking the kids.

"Cut the shit. You always got us running down here over dumb shit. He don't want you girl. Move on." Me and the other two cops were shaking our heads because like I said, it's always the same thing. They know our situation, they know about the court orders and her crazy antics. It never goes the way she wants, and her ass starts throwing a tantrum like she is now.

"I'm coming for my kids."

"Tarshay if you go to his house, I will arrest you for trespassing."

"Really Mark?"

"Yes really. Look at what you're doing in front of the kids." He pointed to my daughter crying and my son looking scared as hell.

"Let me take them home."

"We got this." We have each other a pound and went our separate ways. What a fucking day?

*********************

"Can you play this board? It's really hard." I heard my son ask and assumed he was talking to me until I looked over and saw Ro standing in the kitchen taking pots out to cook.

When we got here, I fed them lunch and turned a movie on. Not too long after they both fell asleep and I guess I did too. Now I'm sitting here on the couch watching Ro try and play the game Junior asked her to and my daughter in her lap. This is the type of peace a nigga supposed to have. I'm not saying Ro don't have a crazy side because we're still learning each other but right now she doesn't.

"When did you get here?"

"Hold on babe. I almost got it." I took my daughter out her hand and laughed as her and Junior started yelling over the game.

"It's a scam Junior. Let me finish cooking and I'll try again." She handed him back the game and kissed his cheek. I think he has a crush on her and why not? Aphrodite is beautiful and any man would be a fool not to see it. It's another reason my ex probably don't like her.

I'm not into looks when it comes to a woman I wanna be with. Yes, Aphrodite is gorgeous but it's not the only reason I fell for her. We have funny and intelligent conversations, we both have conceited ways about ourselves but overall, we mesh well together.

"I guess you staying the night?" I put my daughter down and wrapped my arms around her waist.

"I guess so." She turned and pecked my lips.

"Get used to be here because I don't see you leaving me alone anytime soon."

"Whatever." She smacked my arm and started laughing.

I went to check on the kids and wait for her to finish making us dinner. A nigga could get used to coming home to this.

# Yariah

"What do you want mother?" I spoke with venom in voice answering the phone for her. After seeing her at the rehab a while back and she tried to discredit my father, I haven't spoken to her. My father on the other hand has and went to see her twice. He claims she's doing better but I could care less.

"Can you come see me Riah?" I laughed hard as hell in the phone.

"I'm serious Riah. I need to talk to you." She sounded hurt but then again no one can hurt her. She's the one who instilled the pain in our household.

"Hi, Ms. Perry. This is Dr. Clayton over here at the rehab." I turned my face up because if this doctor is on the phone it only means they want some sorta intervention. I'm really not beat.

"What can I do for you?" I put the phone on speaker and laid back in the bed as Leek started massaging my feet.

"I think we've had some breakthrough with your mom and the next step is to include her family in one of the meetings."

"Ummm." I slightly moaned when Leek stuck my toes in his mouth.

"When is this supposed to take place?" I tried my hardest to speak without given myself away.

"Tomorrow at 2. Your father and siblings have agreed to come if you do."

"Fine!" Leek smiled, let my foot down and started placing soft kisses in between my thighs.

"Great! We'll see you all tomorrow."

"Okkkkkkk." I shouted when his mouth touched my protruding nub. He disconnected the call and tossed the phone on the ground

"About time. Let me taste my sugar." He spoke between him running his tongue in between my folds.

"Sssssss, you know how to make a situation better. Ahhhh fuck?" I gripped the sheets and arched my back as the orgasm begin to brew in my body. It never took him long to get one out.

"That's what I'm here for." He stuck his face back in between my legs and took me to ecstasy like always. Sometimes I get mad at myself for waiting so long to be with him.

Dallas and I had ok sex compared to the way Caleek and I go at it. I mean, he can make me cum and he's a decent size but again, he's no match in the bedroom for Leek. Not to mention, Leek's head game is beyond the best I ever had, and it hasn't been many.

Every now and then, I wonder how Dallas is doing. Not because I want him but because he's tried various times to contact me and I block him. He tried to apologize each time and honestly, I've been over it. The last I heard, he was dating a new chick and already cheated on her but it's just hearsay. I guess he got over me too.

***********************

"I'm very happy to see all of you here today." Dr. Clayton said. She closed the door and took a seat next to my mother. I rolled my eyes and Leek gently pinched my leg. Yes, he came. He wasn't allowing me to come and I have to fight her again.

I glanced around the room and my father was at the table making a cup of coffee. Cazi has his face in the phone and Ro had a look saying she didn't wanna be here either. It's no secret we've all come to the conclusion we're over my mother's antics. She's burned a lotta bridges between the family and I'm not talking about just the ones here. My father's side can't stand her because of the affair she had with my uncle.

Growing up none of us knew why but after revealing the news about me having a different father, I put two and two together. Her side of the family could care less if they spoke to her or not. She stayed in arguments with them too due to her drinking. At this point, we're the only ones who had some sort of involvement with her

"I'm not going to do the whole introduction thing because you're all aware of who's who." She said and pulled out a folder.

"As you all know your mother, and your wife has been here trying to get better. She's had quite a few outbursts. Some violent and others not so much." My mother rolled her eyes.

"Why are we not surprised?" Cazi responded and shook his head.

"This is the exact reason we're here. She'd like to right her wrongs with you all." I busted out laughing and Leek put his head down.

"Listen lady." I crossed my legs and intertwined my hands over my knee

"It's great that you were able to get us all in one room, but you've been played.

"Excuse me." The doctor looked over top of her glasses at me.

"My mother, the one and only Cherisse Perry doesn't know how to apologize, or right her wrongs as you say." I told her. My family looked at me.

"This is why we're here. To leave everything in the past and focus on today and the future." I just looked at her. I hated to do this but I'm gonna have to set my mother off to prove my point.

"Ok let's do it." I uncrossed my legs and felt Leek put his hand on my thigh.

"Start with everyone and save the best for last." I used both of my thumbs and pointed to myself.

I listened to the doctor ask my family a series of questions; they all answered, and my mother sat there looking stupid. She gave these fake ass apologies we all knew meant nothing but continued with the session.

Cazi told my mother she wasn't shit but an abuser and she loved the bottle more than us. It must've hit a nerve because she shed a tear and I do mean one. Ro described her saying me and my brother didn't like her; therefore, it made her turn on us and always have my mom's back. My father described the abuse he endured in so many words and then it was my turn.

It seemed like a never-ending meeting but when I glanced at my phone for the time, it's only been forty minutes.

"Ok mommy dearest. Explain to the doctor here what your issue is with me."

"I don't have an issue with you Yariah. You're the baby in the family and I'm sorry for how I treated you." All eyes were on me.

I took a minute to analyze the situation and the look in my mother's eyes. Nothing about her changed and I knew it. Just like Cazi said the last time, she's doing anything to get outta here.

"I don't believe any of what she's saying." I shrugged my shoulders.

"Why do you feel that way Yariah?" The doctor asked. Poor thing. She's about to get a lot more than she bargained for in this meeting.

"In all honesty, my mother could care less about any of this and probably thinking why is it taking so long; what's the purpose? You see." I stood in front of my mother.

“You may have gone to school to be a doctor Ms. Clayton but when you’ve dealt with the type of abuse this family has, you’ll know when a statement is sincere and when it’s not. None of her apologies are even close to being real.” I smiled at my mother who had a smirk on her face.

“This charade is to get her outta here because frankly my mother doesn’t feel she needs help. Ain’t that right mommy?” I swooped my hair behind my ear.

“This meeting shit is for true alcoholics and that you’re not, because you have, or should I say had a job at CVS. You were better than my father and just because he and I couldn’t take you yelling or fighting us, all this is unnecessary.” I waved my hand around the room.

“Ms. Perry, your mom has...” My mother cut her off.

“You always did think you knew every fucking thing. Why couldn’t you just accept the got damn apology and move on?” I folded my arms against my chest. My mom got out the chair and Caleek pulled me back.

“Come on mama. Show her what you’re really like. Don’t hold back.” I taunted.

“FUCK YOU! YOU’RE A STUPID BITCH JUST LIKE YOUR SISTER. RUNNING BEHIND THESE NIGGAS AND A’INT MAKING NO MONEY. I MEAN GOD GAVE YOU A PUSSY FOR THAT.”

“Cherisse that’s enough.” Dr. Clayton tried to intervene.

“No doctor. Let her finish.” Cazi said and smirked. We all knew she’d break because it’s not in her to be nice.

“And my precious son. Your stupid ass done went and had a fucking baby by a stripper. Does your wife know yet? I mean you should find out if she’ll be ok playing stepmom.” Ro and I both snapped our necks.

"Cazi please tell me she's making that up." My brother was so mad, Caleek and my father had to hold him back

"SECURITY! SECURITY!" The doctor shouted. It was the best thing for her to do right now.

"Oh yea that's your best friend Yariah. Whelp, you better tell her she will never bear his first child; that's if she can have any." I tried to break free from Ro who had to hold me back with one of the security dudes.

"Yo, my man. Back the fuck up." I heard Caleek say.

"Get Mrs. Perry out of here right now." The doctor instructed and one of the guys grabbed her arm.

"I'll be home soon baby, and you can make sweet love to me." She blew my father a kiss.

"I thought his dick was too big and you couldn't cum. Take your dry ass pussy in the back." I shouted.

"It ain't that dry. Is it Caleek?" We all turned around.

"Yo, Cherisse don't try and put me in yo shit. Tha fuck outta here."

"It was funny seeing their faces tho. Tootles y'all." She waved and the door closed. I was so mad my hands were shaking, body trembling and the worst of it, is all I could think of is Amara.

# *Cazi*

"Well that was some meeting." The lady looked disheveled. Her hair was a little outta place, glasses crooked, and she was sweating like a damn slave. Her under pits were so wet, when she lifted her arms you saw a wet spot.

"You wanted to have the meeting and it wouldn't have been fair not to show you who Cherisse Perry truly is." I said and saw both of my sisters grabbing their things. Caleek had a *oh shit you in trouble* look on his face and my father didn't know what to say.

The day Caleek opened the envelope with the results in them, we never got the chance to see what they were because the little boy jumped in front of my truck. I can't even tell you where the paper is and to be honest, I didn't care at the moment. Yea, I should know if it's my daughter and I'm wasting spending more time with her by not knowing. I guess I'll have to contact LabCorp and talk to my peoples. I'm sure she can print me up a copy or give me the results.

"I wasn't expecting things to escalate. Your mom showed much improvement here and I'm afraid if this didn't happen, once she was on the outside it would've happened again."

"At this point Ms. Clayton you can release her."

"What?" She seemed surprised.

"I know this is a place where she has to complete the program, but I'm done paying. It's obvious not even a facility can change her."

"Mr. Perry."

"It's not you Ms. Clayton because I'm sure everyone here did their job. However; I know my mother and as bad as I thought she could change, she can't and won't."

"I'm sorry this is happening in your family." I shrugged my shoulders.

"I'm going to keep her here but the minute she requests to leave again, I'll make it happen."

"It's whatever but do me a favor, and don't contact and of us. As you can see we don't wanna be bothered." She nodded and I rushed out to catch my sisters before they left.

"Riah, it's not like that." I tried to talk to my sisters, but they were both walking fast as hell.

"YARIAH AND APHRODITE STOP!" I barked and they both froze. They knew to listen if I raised my voice.

"I'll be in the truck Riah." Leek told her and stepped off. My father stood next to me. I have yet to tell him because like I said, until I read the results, I'm still unsure. No need to get anyone riled up yet.

"Is mommy lying?" I leaned against my truck and stared in the sky.

"Yes and no." I heard one of them suck their teeth.

"When I cheated, I didn't use a condom and..." I blew my breath.

"She had a baby and said it was mine."

"Hold up. The stripper woman is the chick?" Riah blurted out. It wasn't a secret who I cheated with.

"You have a child by a stripper?" Ro chimed in.

"I don't know."

"Cazi you can't have a child out there with no father." Riah had an attitude when she said it.

"I took the test and just as I went to read the results, we ended up in the shootout. I don't even know where the paper went."

"This is gonna kill Amara, especially after what she went through." Riah responded with sincerity.

"I know which is another reason why I wasn't in a rush to get the test and then took my time opening the envelope."

"Shit! How the fuck am I gonna tell Amara?" Riah paced back and forth.

"Let me tell her sis." She stopped and looked at me.

"It has to come from me."

"Fine. Let me know when you tell her because someone's going to need to be around." Riah was pissed and she had every right to be. Amara is like her other sister.

"Cazi you know what she went through during the break up. This is bad." Ro reminded me.

"Which is why I'm not until I get down to LabCorp and get a duplicate of the results. The minute I know, she will too." They both hugged me.

"Is it a girl or boy?" Ro questioned.

"A girl. Her name is Destiny."

"I know it sounds fucked up because of what Amara's going to go through but I can't wait to meet her." Ro said. I slightly smiled.

"Sis, I haven't even met her."

"WHAT?" Riah shouted.

"She approached me at the mall and tried but I cursed her out because Amara was with me and I didn't know if she was lying. I only took the test because your mother claimed she resembled me."

"Mommy." Ro asked.

"Evidently, her brother is the worker Caleek beat up at the reception." Riah snapped her neck.

"Don't get upset. He didn't know either."

"This is crazy." Riah shouted walking to her car. I didn't even chase after her and quickly sent a message to Leek. I told him to tell her not to say anything and I'm going to get the results.

"If I were you, I'd tell her now. She's in a rehab and can't try anything." Ro said and kissed my cheek.

"I don't want her in anymore pain tho."

"Oh, this is definitely gonna hurt but she loves you Cazi. When she took you back, she forgave everything. Well no one knew a baby was involved but it is what it is." She shrugged and went to her car. I hopped in the truck with my father who still had a blank look on his face.

"This entire situation is crazy. First your mother and now this baby." He patted my shoulder.

"If that's your baby I wanna meet my granddaughter." My father couldn't wait for grandkids.

"You got it." I started the truck and pulled off.

*********************

"I'm here to see Amara Perry." I told the receptionist at the desk. It's been three weeks since the accident and I'm just making it here. It's not that I didn't wanna come, I just couldn't look her in the face knowing the possibility of me having an outside child is there. I'm fucked up over what she contemplated doing which is why I didn't wanna cause anymore hurt. Unfortunately, I have to tell her. Plus, I had to make changes at the house for her.

"She's in the therapist room." The woman pressed the button at the door and told me what room to go in.

"You're doing great Mrs. Perry." I heard opening the door. I leaned on the side and stared at my wife trying her hardest to walk again. The woman looked up and smiled. I put my finger to my lips, walked behind Amara and removed the walker.

"What the...?" I heard panic in Amara's voice.

"Keep going." I told her.

"I can't Cazi. I need the walker." I grabbed her waist gently and held her tight before moving in front of her.

"I won't let you fall." She nodded and took a small step. I could tell it hurt but she continued.

"Wow, Mrs. Perry we should've gotten him here sooner. And who are you sir?" The therapist extended her hand.

"Mr. Perry." She looked at Amara who shrugged her shoulders.

"I'm sure my wife mentioned us not being together." I lifted her face with my finger.

"When I said til death do us part, I meant it." I gave her a look she knew too well. I never had to yell to get my point across. Amara swallowed hard and the therapist didn't know what to say.

"Ummm ok. That's enough walking for today. We don't need Mrs. Perry putting too much weight on her pelvis." The woman pushed a cushioned chair that reclined over. After she removed the belts that connected to some bar, she carefully placed Amara on it.

"Would you like to push her to the room?" The therapist asked. Amara remained quiet.

"Sure. Should I put her in the bed or leave her in this chair?"

"It's totally up to her. Nice meeting you." She waved and walked over to another patient.

Amara directed me down the hall to her room but not without cutting her eyes and sucking her teeth at the nurses staring and smiling. She hated for other women to stare or even offer a compliment. She's very laid back and quiet, but I still noticed the aggravation it causes.

When we got in the room, I pushed her by the window and asked if she wanted to get in bed. She gave me attitude and I wasn't even mad. She expected for me to kiss her ass for leaving and not visiting and she had every right to. I knew how she was doing through Riah, but I should've been here.

"Where's your ring?" I felt myself getting upset. Here she told me get the marriage annulled and I didn't. Shit, I still had my ring on.

"Why are you here?" I saw the hurt on her face but it's time to deal with our shit. At least I know she can't run out when I tell her.

# *Amara*

I hated that my husband was so damn fine. Women gawked over him wherever we went and regardless of him not addressing it, it still pissed me off. All the damn, *he fine, she don't know what to do with all that* and the tons of disrespectful things I hear gets to be too much.

Now he's sitting in front of me looking sexy as hell. My body reacted to his touch in the therapy room and right now I wish he would leave so I can handle myself. Hell no I'm not ashamed that I play with myself. If I can't have who I want, then I'll gladly do it myself. Ain't no need to be horny and mad. Shit, get yourself off and take a nap. Trust, you'll feel better when you wake up.

"Where's your ring?" He asked a second time and I shrugged my shoulders.

"Tha fuck you mean, you don't know?"

"I thought you wanted to get the marriage annulled and..."

"Those were your words Amara, not mine."

"I just thought since I failed as a girlfriend and wife, you'd wanna move on." My eyes started watering.

"What the hell are you talking about? You didn't fail at shit."

"Cazi, I know it's in the past but it's the only reason I could come up with as to why you cheated. As far as being your wife, I failed because you want kids and I'm struggling to do that." The tears started racing down my face by now.

"Why spend the rest of your life with a woman who can't give you everything you want?" He bent down in front of me.

"Amara, if you failed at anything, I would've never married you."

“But it was under false pretenses. I didn’t want you to leave me.” I cried.

“It doesn’t matter anymore Amara. We were meant to be anyway. You just pushed the process up.”

“Cazi, I’m so sorry. I should’ve told you about the abortion. Again, I was petrified you wouldn’t want me. Can you forgive me?” I wiped my eyes.

“I forgave you the minute you described what happened. Amara, I’m sorry you felt there wasn’t a way out and that I’d leave you if another child was involved.”

“You would’ve stayed around?” I asked to hear what he’d say. I was curious.

“It happened when we weren’t together. You know how bad I fought to get you back. Of course I would’ve accepted the child.” He passed me some tissue.

“Amara things happened between us we can’t dwell on. I fucked up, which made you do things you’d never do otherwise. If anyone should apologize, it’s me.”

“You already did Cazi.” He ran the back of his hand down the side of my face and smiled.

“I have to tell you something.” I don’t know why but the way he said it sent chills down my spine.

“Are you ok?”

“I’m fine.”

“Then what’s wrong?” I saw him struggling to speak.

“I ran into the stripper not too long ago.” I sucked my teeth.

“Please don’t tell me you slept with her again.”

“HELL NO!” He shouted; making me jump.

"Let me guess. She started reminiscing on the night y'all had." I still get upset about the affair he had with her.

"Something like that. Amara she..."

"WE'RE HAVING A BOYYYYYYY!" Yariah ran in yelling. She had a picture in her hand and Caleek came strolling in behind her.

"Congratulations. I'm so happy for you. I hope you not naming him after his father." I joked.

"Don't play me Amara." Caleek laughed it off.

"What y'all got going on?" Riah asked and stared at Cazi.

"Nothing. Your brother was about to mention the shit with the stripper. Do you know she approached him and started reminiscing? She better not let me catch her because I'm beating her ass again." I noticed Yariah and Caleek staring at Cazi.

"What's going on? FUCKKKKKKK!" I cried out when I tried to move in the chair. I may be walking here and there but my body stiffens up quick and it's a bitch tryna move.

"You ok?" Cazi rushed to my side.

"I'm fine. Can you ask the nurse to bring me some pain medication?" They all looked at me.

"I'm not addicted or anything like that. I told them I only want it after therapy. I deal with the pain the rest of the time."

"You ready to go Mrs. Perry?" The doctor walked in with a grin on his face.

"Home?" I questioned.

"Yes. Your husband has been working with us daily on getting you home. Here's your discharge papers and the medication was sent over to your pharmacy.

"Cazi?"

"My wife has been here too long. She needs to be home in her own bed." He said with finality.

"But therapy and..."

"You're gonna have the same therapy sessions here four times a week like you've been doing. One of those days you'll have services at home in the pool. Trust me, it works wonders." The doctor said and finished going over everything with me.

I'm happy to leave but I didn't forget the looks on all their faces. Whatever it is they're hiding is gonna come up and I pray it's not him saying it's another woman.

************************

"Oh wow!" I was amazed at the house.

In order for me to leave the hospital, I had to lay in the backseat and Cazi drove extremely slow. The bumps were a bitch, but it was worth it to come home. I was tired of those rehabilitation walls.

"It took some time to make changes, but you should be good until you're better." He walked behind me with the walker.

I glanced at the small ramp that led outside in the back. There was a railing and I noticed some things by the pool. I turned slowly and there was a small reclining chair similar to the one in the rehab. He helped me in it and walked me to one of the downstairs rooms. He opened the door and there was a brand-new bedroom set.

"I had one of those tub/ shower things in the bathroom since you can't stand long." He showed it to me, and it was the tub with the door. All you had to do is step in and sit. It's mostly used for old and handicapped people, but I appreciated the fact he went through all this.

"This is too much."

"Nothing is too much for you Amara and when it's time for us to have kids, we will."

"Come here." I gestured with my finger. I placed him in front of me and undid his jeans.

"Amara you don't have to." I stopped and stared.

"You been with someone else?"

"Never but you just got home and oh fuckkkkk!" He moaned out when his dick touched the back of my throat. Not even two minutes later, he exploded.

"I can't have sex yet, but I'll satisfy you in other ways."

"Shit." He fell back on the bed and I started laughing.

"You needed that huh?"

"You have no idea babe. Fuck I missed you." He said and gently lifted me on the bed.

"I wanna make love to you so bad right now."

"Please don't cheat because you have to wait."

"I won't Amara. I swear, I'll never cheat on you again." He kissed me with so much passion my body reacted and as bad as I wanted him, the pain from me tryna lift my leg was too bad.

"I'll wait forever if I need to." He whispered and laid next to me.

"I'm happy you're home."

"Me too baby. Me too." We both laid there in silence for a few minutes. I asked him to put me in the bath because even though he couldn't touch me, my pussy was still wet.

Afterwards, I wanted to eat and watch movies with my husband and that's exactly what we did. I pray nothing or no one messes up our happiness.

## *Tasheem*

"How do you plead Ms. Perry?" The judge asked the Yariah bitch.

It's been over a month and we're just now getting the bitch arraigned. She should've been here, but her lawyer kept postponing; talking about he needed more time. Granted it was last minute that we filed the charges, but it shouldn't have stopped the arraignment. I know Caleek and Cazi had everything to do with it

"Not guilty." I sucked my teeth when she answered.

"Ms. Compton, I understand your frustration but I'm going to ask that you refrain from any comments, eye rolling and teeth sucking in my courtroom. Are we clear?" The judge said in a stern voice.

"Yes." I glanced on the other side and Yariah had a straight face.

"Now Ms. Perry, I know you pleaded *not guilty,* but I want to go over the charges again just to be clear. If at any time you feel the need to change your plea let me know." The judge looked at her as he spoke.

"The charges are as follows; conspiracy to commit a crime by setting up an ambush. Kidnapping, abduction, loss of life..."

"Loss of life?" Yariah questioned him.

"Yes. Ms. Compton was pregnant at the time and at some point, she miscarried." I saw her snap her neck at Caleek. I guess he didn't tell her.

"Can I continue?"

"Yes, I'm sorry."

"Where was I? Ok. Arson, the murders of four different men and auto theft."

"Auto theft?" She questioned him again.

"Yes. The alleged getaway vehicle was stolen."

"That's a lotta charges." She had the nerve to say.

"Yes it is. I'm going to ask again. How to you plead?"

"Not guilty." Her lawyer whispered something in her ear and turned to look at the judge.

"Your honor, my client is requesting a restraining order against Ms. Compton." He took his glasses off and stared in my direction.

"Why would Ms. Perry need a restraining order on a woman she allegedly did all these things to?" I put my head down.

"What's going on Tasheem?" My lawyer asked.

"Judge. May I?" Her lawyer asked if he could show him a video on the iPad. He watched whatever it was and barked at my lawyer to stand before him. After a little whispering both lawyers returned to their seat.

"Ms. Compton, in a brief description I need to know why you attacked this woman, twice I may add, at a restaurant? Then you attempted to get her arrested for an assault you provoked." I didn't say anything.

"Ms. Compton, I can't imagine what you went through over the course of time in which you were taken; however, it doesn't give you the right to go around attacking people. And furthermore, in my opinion and I'm speaking strictly from the paperwork in front of me. I'm not sure you have the correct person."

"Excuse me! That bitch is the one who did this." I pointed to Yariah as I heard the gavel slam on his table

"You have every right to feel the way you do, and this case will go on when a date is set, but Ms. Compton what you need to do, is put whatever hatred you have towards this woman to the side and take a deeper look. Why would this woman do it? Did you see her at any time while you were captured? Did she gain anything keeping you away besides a man you used to have? And last but not least, be sure this is the woman because as much time as you're spending accusing her with this circumstantial evidence, you're allowing the real culprit to roam free. Court dismissed until the trial date." Everyone stood.

"And Ms. Compton, if I hear you went on an attacking spree again, you'll be the one locked up until the trial. Do you understand?" I put my head down.

"DO YOU UNDERSTAND?"

"Yes sir."

"Perfect." He walked into his office and closed the door.

"Tasheem what the hell is going on? Why did you attack her? I'm no longer gonna represent you if this is how you'll behave." My lawyer went on and on as I picked my things up. I ignored her and walked over to Caleek who had his arms around Yariah.

"Caleek." I didn't shout or yell.

"Bitch, if you lay one finger on my girl, I'll beat your ass in this courtroom." I froze in place.

"Leek, it's ok. I'm gonna wait with Cazi." She kissed him, rolled her eyes and walked out.

"What the fuck you want?" He stared me down and the entire time I thought of how perfect we used to be.

"Ummmm. I was thinking." I started fidgeting with my hands. It's what I did when I'm nervous.

"About?" He circled his finger to rush me.

"Since I'm not sure exactly what happened to me, is there anyone who can make me remember?"

"Tha fuck you mean, you don't remember?" He had bass in his voice.

"I tried to tell you at the diner."

"Your fault for acting stupid. Keep going."

"Well the entire time, I was heavily sedated or something. I don't remember who had me, or anything." He gripped my arm, pulled me out the door and in a corner.

"Bitch, you accusing my girl and don't know what the fuck really happened?"

"Caleek she's the only one who hated me." He laughed.

"Riah has never hated you Tasheem and you would've known that had you not been so ignorant. Yes, we had feelings towards each other, but we've never done anything sexual until months after I thought you passed. Now you're standing here telling me you have no idea what went down, yet tryna send he to jail."

"WHAT?" Cazi shouted. We weren't far from where they stood. Caleek explained to him what I said.

"There's a woman who does hypnosis and from what I hear, she's very good." Cazi said and looked through his phone.

"But the doctor said with all the drugs in my body I may never know."

"Regardless of how drugged up you were, it had to be times where it wore off. Within those seconds or minutes, you should have seen some things or heard voices." Caleek responded.

"We all know Yariah isn't gonna do a day in jail." Cazi said and gave me a fake smile.

"Anyway, were gonna help you this one time because whoever did it is still out there, and I'll be damned if they kidnap my sister and nephew."

"Nephew?" Leek smiled.

"Yup. My son is in her stomach." I rolled my eyes.

"Go to this woman and see if she can help, otherwise; I'd try really hard to remember because this trial ain't even gonna happen." Cazi ran her number off to me.

"Caleek, what happens if I remember?"

"Call me and we'll go from there."

"You're gonna help me." He walked in my face.

"I shouldn't help you with a fucking thing after you attacked Riah. The only reason I am is because she's scared the same thing is gonna happen to her for being with me." I sucked my teeth.

"Be mad all you want but it's the truth. If my girl told me to let you suffer, I would've. Now go see the woman and hit me up." He left me standing there stuck on stupid.

At this point, I don't even care because he's going to help. He's right too. What if the person tries to take me again?

**********************

"Hi Ms. Compton." The hypnosis lady who Cazi sent me to spoke. I shook her hand and followed her inside the back. It took me a week to come here because I was nervous and scared of what I may find out.

Her office was very eclectic and unlike any I've ever seen. She had incense burning, it was a tad bit dark and once we went in the room, there was a couch like thing in the middle of the floor with a chair directly across. She offered me a seat and told me to make myself comfortable. I needed to feel relaxed in order for it work correctly. I shook my body, tried to crack my neck and knuckles to look like I knew something.

Unfortunately, I twisted my neck the wrong way and thought I pulled a muscle and my knuckles were cracked before I got out the car, therefore they made no noise. The lady looked at me and smiled. I'm sure she could tell how uncomfortable I was. I wanted to know what happened to me, but I'm scared to find out at the same time if that makes sense.

"Ok. Let's start off with you telling me some things about yourself. Your likes and dislikes, where you grew up, things of that sort." As I began telling her she made two cups of coffee and offered me one. Being on edge with everything, I declined.

"Ok. This is what's going to happen." She had me lay back on the couch.

"I'm doing it the old-fashioned way with this symbolic locket. You're going to follow it and count backwards from one hundred." I nodded.

"The first thing I want you to do is go back to the night you told Caleek about the pregnancy, right before the attack." I looked at her.

"Yea, he gave me a short run down." She smiled. I blew my breath and shook my hands.

"Ok I'm ready." I followed the locket and began to count backwards. Before I knew it, I was in the restaurant talking to Caleek. I guess this shit does work.

*"Baby, remember when we spoke on having kids?" I told Leek who just handed his menu to the waitress. He proposed at my party and we were still out celebrating.*

*"Yea. Did my sperm work?" I threw my head back laughing.*

*"Yes.*

*"Really?" His face lit up.*

*"I went to the doctors this morning with Amara and saw the baby."*

*"Where's the photo?"*

*"I was gonna tell you at home, but I couldn't wait. It's at my mom's house. We can pick it up on the way home."*

*"I'm about to be a father." He scooted closer to me and rubbed my belly. The two of us ate dinner and went out to celebrate at the club. We were all over one another in there and decided to go home and fuck the hell outta each other.*

*On the way, when we were stopped at a red light cars came outta nowhere and Leek told me to relax. Our doors were opened, and we were snatched out. He started whooping a couple of the guys ass. They pistol whipped him and tossed us in the back of a van. I had his head in my lap as he laid unconscious Well, he looked it anyway.*

*The doors opened not too long after and we were drug inside some warehouse. There were a ton of people inside and even though Leek prepared me for this, I wasn't ready when the guy punched me in the face and knocked me over still attached to the chair.*

*I was able to finagle my way out the knot, grabbed the gun out the guys pocket who had his back turned and started shooting. Bodies dropped and somehow, I was shot in the leg and someone fell on top of me. I heard a door being kicked in and prayed it was to rescue us. Cazi yelled and I heard Leek asking where I was.*

*My body was being lifted by someone and placed in a car. I figured it was one of the guys with Cazi and laid there praying we got to a hospital quick. The pain in my leg was unbearable and I wanted it to go away. I let my hands go to my stomach and closed my eyes. A few minutes later there was an explosion and it's all I remember.*

"You're doing great Tasheem. I pulled you out to get some water because your voice seemed dry." The lady passed me a closed water bottle and started texting on her phone. I didn't even know I was speaking out loud.

"I'm ready." I slammed my head back on the pillow.

"I was thinking we should finish this tomorrow. Give you some time to get it together."

"NO! I wanna finish." She gave me a weird stare and came back over to do that thing again with the locket.

To be honest, I wanted to know where my child was and who did this. I wouldn't sleep if I didn't get it done. She ran the locket in my face and had me count backwards again.

*"Where am I?" I opened my eyes and noticed my hands and legs were strapped to a bed. There was an IV in my arm and you could hear what sounded like a monitor behind me. Nothing was in here except a television and a chair across from me.*

*"HELP! HELP ME!" I shouted and the door opened. In walked someone dressed in black with their face was covered.*

*"Your stupid boyfriend got away. Where's the money?" The unknown woman spoke.*

*"Money? What money?"*

*WHAP! She smacked fire from my ass.*

*"His money. Where is it? My cousin said you'd know where it was." I had no idea what money she's referring to. If it's Caleek's, I definitely couldn't tell her because he never told me how much money he had. Whoever this is and her cousin must've assumed I did because we were together.*

*"I don't know what you're talking about."*

*"All the man power we had to kidnap y'all stupid ass and you're telling me you don't know?"*

*"I don't." This time she punched me with so much force it knocked me completely out. The attacks went on for months but each time I woke up, instead of hitting me, the woman who later stopped coming, and the man, injected something into the IV to make me sleep. I can't even tell you how long I was there.*

*"GET UP!" Someone yelled and I felt the straps being removed from my arms and legs. I looked and his face was covered too.*

*"HURRY UP BEFORE THEY COME BACK."*

*"I can't move. My body is weak." He lifted me off the stretcher, carried me up some steps and to a truck.*

*"Who are you and why are you helping me?" He put the key in the ignition.*

*"Let's just say the bitch who put you here owed me a favor and never came through. Plus, with TJ running around you need to go to him."*

*"TJ?" I questioned.*

*"I'm dropping you off at a hospital. They'll know who you are because your information is in here."*

*"WAIT! How long have I been here? Who's the woman that did this?" He ignored each question.*

*"Remember what I said." He helped me out the truck and placed me on the sidewalk next to a hospital.*

*"I can't remember anything," I told him tryna recollect something.*

*"It's because they were giving you a drug to erase your memory but they stupid because after a while it will wear off."*

*"Why did they do this to me?"*

*"Money is the root of all evil ma. Your man is rich, and they want what he has; especially your ex."*

*"My ex."*

*"Yup. I have to go. Here's the envelope and find TJ soon as you can. He's not in a good space."*

*"Who's TJ?" He pulled his phone out and what he said next, had me at a loss for words.*

"WAKE UP TASHEEM! TASHEEM ARE YOU OK?" I heard the lady screaming. She was shaking my body so hard my neck went back and forth. I couldn't open my eyes. I didn't want to because I needed him to tell me.

"TASHEEM!"

*SPLASH!* She tossed water in my face.

"OH MY GOD!" I hopped up and started grabbing my things.

"What's wrong?"

"I have to go."

"Tasheem you're drenched in sweat. What's wrong? What did you see?" I grabbed the doorknob and turned to her.

"My son."

## *Aphrodite*

"We're fine Bongi." I spoke in the phone.

"You sure because Aleese can be a lot." I looked down at his daughter who was passed out in Amara's lap.

"I'm sure babe. Just hurry up so I can go for a ride later." I had a grin on my face. I loved having sex with him.

"Bet. I'll call as soon as I'm done with your brother."

"Ok." We both said I love you and hung up.

I stared at Amara and how loving she was towards Aleese. My brother messed up real bad and I can only hope for his sake she sticks around after he tells her.

"You want me to take her?" I tossed my phone on the couch.

"No, I'm ok."

"You sure? I know you're doing a lot better, but I don't wanna put any pressure on you. Cazi would kill me if you got hurt again." She smiled and ran her hand down Aleese face.

Amara has been doing much better since coming home from the rehab. Cazi refused to let anyone come over unless she mentioned it. He didn't want anyone upsetting her or making her walk and he wasn't there to catch her if she fell. He's always been overprotective of Amara but now he's worse. I know it's because of the baby issue too but I would never tell. That's his job and I hope it's soon because each day he's missing out on more time.

"He's such a brat when it comes to me. Sometimes I think he blames himself for what happened." I sat next to her.

"Yea well, we both know once he finds the person it's over."

"I know." She smiled again and handed me the baby while she went to the bathroom. I offered to help her walk, and she almost ripped my head off. She no longer uses the walker and claims the cane is fine. I put Aleese down and checked on Junior who was in their bedroom playing a video game.

Ever since Bongi and I been together and he took the kids from Tarshay, they've been a fixture in my life. I would love to have kids one day but not right now. My sisters having one, Bongi has two and Cazi is definitely gonna get Amara pregnant. And let's not forget the possibility of him already having one. I'm on the pill at the moment and I make sure no dose is missed because once we stopped using condoms, he never pulls out.

"What ya doing?" I asked Junior who was lying on his stomach.

"Trying to pass the dragons. You wanna try?" He handed me the remote and the two of us stayed in there for about an hour defeating all the bad guys.

"Hey. I'm a little tired. Do you two mind if I lay in here with y'all?" Amara asked and came over to the bed.

"You don't have to ask to lay on your own bed." I told her.

"I know but he's so into the game and..." Junior cut her off.

"No aunt Amara. Here lay next to me." He moved over and patted the bed. He started calling everyone aunty. Evidently, my brother and Caleek been his uncle.

*DING DONG!*

"I'll get it." I tried to avoid her from walking too much.

"I got it. Can you check on Aleese again? She was still asleep in the playpen." I walked out behind her and went in the living room.

"Hello Amara." I stopped when my mother's voiced boomed through the doorway.

"Hey mother in law. How can I help you?" I could hear my mother asking if she could come in. Being the nice person Amara is, she allowed her access.

"Hey daughter."

"Mother. How are you out?" I questioned her presence because she's supposed to be in rehab.

"Well your brother stopped paying and let's just say, when the money ran out, I wasn't paying for shit. Damn this TV is big." She ran closer to the entertainment stand.

"Hey Babe." I answered for Bongi.

"Hey. I'm gonna be late. Can you take the kids home and I'll wake you up to take that ride when I get there?" I busted out laughing.

"It better be worth the wait."

"Always sexy. You just be ready to stay up half the night."

"Mmmm, I can't wait." We said our goodbyes and as I started getting the kids ready to go, I couldn't help but overhear my mother on the phone telling someone where she was and that's it's no problem stopping by.

"Amara, I don't wanna leave you here with her but it's after eight and Bongi wants me to take the kids home." I looked at my mother who had a sneaky grin on her face.

"Matter of fact, why don't you come with me? Cazi will pick you up on the way in."

"It's ok Ro. Your mom is harmless to me." I was stuck at her response. My mom has never really been mean to Amara but I don't trust her. She stopped by for something.

"You sure?" I put the seatbelt over Junior and buckled Aleese in her seat too.

"I'll be fine." She kissed my cheek and bid me farewell.

On the way to Bongi's, I felt like someone was following me. Every turn I made, so did this car. At the light, the car would move up to me so close I thought their front bumper was touching my back one.

As we turned on Bongi's street the car sped up behind me and before I could move out the way, it pushed us into his front gate. The airbag deployed and my face banged against the window. I heard the kids screaming but my body was stuck. I couldn't move, nor turn my neck to see if they were ok.

"Junior you're gonna be ok." I said out loud hoping he could hear me. All of a sudden, the back door opened, and he stopped crying. A few minutes later Aleese stopped crying. All I had to do now is wait for the person to help me.

"You thought making Bongi fall in love would excuse you from my wrath?"

"Tarshay?" I whispered because I was now tryna stay awake. My head was pounding, and blood was trickling down.

"You bitches will learn that even though I don't want Bongi, no other woman will have him either." She had this wicked laugh.

"If you don't want him why are you going through all this?"

"Because it's fun."

"You're not gonna get away with this."

"That's where you're wrong Ro. You have no idea how many women he had to pay off because I've scared them away or almost took their life. Somehow, he kept you protected up until tonight. So if you wanna be mad, be mad at him." She was laughing hysterically.

"Oh, and just so he knows it was me, let me leave my signature."

"AHHHHHHH!" She began stabbing me in my arm, side and legs.

"Now watch this." She put her phone on speaker and started talking when a woman said hello.

"Hi this is…" She made up some fake name.

"I just witnessed this woman driving erratically and she crashed into a gate. Oh my God, there kids in the car."

"Are the kids ok ma'am?"

"Is that liquor?"

"Ma'am are the kids ok?" The woman asked again.

"I'm not sure." She finished talking to the lady and hung up.

"Dammit. Now I have to put the kids back in your car." How she mad when she doing all this extra shit?

"See you soon Ro and it won't be the way you want."

"Mommy what are you doing?" Junior asked.

"Get in the damn car and stop asking questions." I could hear him asking more anyway.

"Drunk driving with my kids in your car is gonna make Bongi kill you." She whispered in my ear and a few seconds later, my eyes closed.

# *Yariah*

"It took me forever to find you." I turned to hear Lori's voice.

"Bitch where the fuck you been?" Caleek barked. We were walking out the movie theatre. The new Spider-Man came out and since he's a closet comic book freak, he dragged me here to see it.

"Is that anyway to speak to the woman you almost spent a year with?" Caleek opened the door for me to walk out.

I've never been the person who believed in premonitions or eerie feelings, but something wasn't right. I glanced around the parking lot and things seemed to be ok, but my stomach was doing flips. It could've been my son moving, or the fact Lori showed up. How did she know we were here anyway? Is she alone? And where the hell is her stomach? Her shit is flat as hell.

"I've tried to contact your stupid ass. Did you have the baby?" She tossed her head back laughing hysterically.

"Caleek we both know I'm not mother material."

"I don't know what you are besides crazy. Get in the truck Riah." He hit the alarm and opened the door.

"Where's the baby?" He questioned again.

"I terminated it." He closed my door but I surely rolled the window down to hear.

"Word?" I thought his response would've been angry or upset.

"Are you gonna kill me for it?" The smile on her face made me turn around.

"Why would I kill you for that? I doubt it was mine and you know I never wanted a kid with you. Stop playing stupid." When Caleek wasn't tryna hear anyone's bullshit you could tell by his response. Lori knew too because she was tryna egg him on to see if he'd get angrier.

"Baby, who is that?" I asked when some tall, dark-skinned guy came strolling up.

"It must be Tone." He answered and kept his eyes on Lori. I immediately sent a message to Cazi and told him to get here. I sent one to Ro as well so she could tell Bongi.

"Let me ask you this Lori."

"What?" I looked up when I heard the click. The Tone guy had a gun placed on the back of Leek's head. I didn't know what to do.

"Was it worth it?" Leek stood there with his arms folded and unbothered.

"What?" She reached behind and pulled out her own gun.

"Setting up the ambush, and kidnapping me and Tasheem?" I gasped.

"Actually, it wasn't because we didn't get any money from you. I mean we definitely reaped the benefits from the money you gave the reverend. Too bad he didn't make it to the bank to cash the check." I covered my mouth when Lori revealed in so many words that the reverend's dead. Caleek turned and now Tone's gun was on his forehead.

"And Tone. You helped her and still didn't get money or the girl."

"FUCK YOU NIGGA! YOU SWEAR YOU'RE BETTER THAN US."

"Nah, you think that, which is why you and this idiot." He pointed to Lori.

"I'm offended." She said and put her hand on her chest as if she really were.

"You and this idiot kept the fact you're cousins a secret."

"Oh shit." I yelled out by accident and Lori put her gun on my forehead through the window. I remembered Leek telling me the people who abducted them were related.

"It took me a minute to realize it was you two fucktards that pulled the shit off and I'm impressed. Who knew you had it in you to set this up?" He turned around.

"And Lori good job with the fake hazel contacts and using the high pitch voice. You threw me off for sure."

"Thank you very much. I worked very hard on my disguise." Was this bitch bragging?

"SHUT THE FUCK UP LORI." Tone yelled.

"Why? He know we did it. Let's just get the keys to his house, take the safe out the wall and leave? We wasted enough time here and since he chose this bitch over me, no need to stay."

"Who the fuck cares if we're related and I didn't get the girl? You and everyone else thought she died." Tone ignored Lori and continued questioning Leek.

"Did you have to kill my brother?" Lori asked and we all looked at her.

"Who's your brother?" I asked not really caring.

"The guy at the house where your brother's baby mama lived." She said it with sarcasm.

"WHAT?" I shouted and she started laughing.

"Oh yea, I forgot. Your brother had a baby and the stripper bitch, I think her name is Simone." She placed her index finger under her chin.

"Anyway, we found out she was blackmailing your bother and even though he didn't know it was her address, we sent her son outside to be a decoy. Long story short, the bitch is dead. A life for a life."

"OH MY GOD! Where are the kids?" Leek just stared at her for some reason.

"Who the fuck cares about those kids? You're next bitch." Leek looked at her with a *yea right* face.

"What do you really want Tone?" Leek had his fist balled up at this point. I knew he wasn't about to let them get him again.

"Everything you have; including the new bitch." Now it was time for Leek to laugh.

"Had you not gotten to the hospital when I tried to run the bitch over with my truck, she was definitely next to be taken." My heart started beating fast when Lori said that.

"Hold up. You're the one who tried to kill me?" I opened the door and stepped out.

"Get back in Riah."

"Yup and had that dumb bitch your brother cheated on, not jumped in the way you'd be somewhere dead or tryna escape like Tasheem did." She thought the shit was hysterically.

"What's going on over there?" You heard someone ask and Tone told them to mind their business or he'd shoot them.

"I'm finished talking. Let's kill them and go." I saw both of them put their finger on the trigger. My instincts kicked in and I threw a punch that landed on Lori's face. Her gun dropped and the bitch had the audacity to scream out. I kept hitting her and stopped when a gun went off.

"LEEEEEEEKKKK!!!!!!!

## *Amara*

"What can I do for you Cherisse?" I closed the door after walking Ro and the kids to the car. I've been doing so much better since the accident and the doctor was right about the water working wonders.

Since the therapist who worked with me in the water was a man, Cazi had to be here when he came. He had a fit and threatened to send him away if I objected. I had to talk him out of it because he was very persistent. He even made sure I wore leggings, a long tank top, and one of his black T-shirt's in the water. The therapist was an older gentleman and scared to death of Cazi. Him and Caleek thought it was funny, but I didn't. Talking about ain't no man gonna be turned on by his wife.

Anyway, each day I progressed, the more I wanted to do. In the mornings, I had Cazi carry me down the steps because I no longer wanted to stay down there. If I wanted a nap and he wasn't here, I'd lay in the downstairs bedroom but that's it. At night, I had him walk behind me up the steps. It hurt like hell but if I didn't do it, I'd always be stuck. I wanted to feel as normal as possible and it's easier going up then it is down.

"I just wanted to stop by and see my daughter in law." I took a seat next to her and sent a text to Cazi mentioning her presence. He didn't have to rush home and even though I told Ro she's harmless, I'm positive she's gonna piss me off. My phone rang immediately after hitting send.

"You ok?" Cazi asked.

"I'm fine." I glanced over at Cherisse who now had a weird look on her face as she stared at her own phone.

"Put me on speaker." I did like he asked.

"What the fuck you doing at my house?" He barked and she looked up. I gave her a fake smile and shrugged my shoulders.

"Son is that anyway to speak to your mother?"

"Tha fuck you want?" He barked again.

"I'm here visiting Cazi that's all damn. Can you hang up so I can fill my daughter in law on what she's been missing?"

"GET THE FUCK OUT MY HOUSE!" This time he shouted.

"Cazi it's fine. I'll see you soon."

"Ma, I swear if you hurt her in any way, I'll break your got damn neck."

"I love you too son." She blew him a kiss and made the loud kissing noise.

"See you later babe."

"I'm on my way." He hung the phone up. I placed it on the coffee table and stared at her. Whatever she planned on telling me must be of significance because she now had a grin on her face.

"I've always loved you for my son Amara. You are the calm to his storm and honestly, you're his everything." I blushed at her response. Cazi and I had a rough patch, but it made us stronger and the accident pushed us away a little. Thankfully, after all that, we're back in a good space.

"Do you think y'all will ever have kids?" Why was she asking me this?

"I believe when God is ready for me to give him some, he'll help out. Why do you ask?"

"It would be ashamed if he stepped out and let another woman carry his child or children because you can't."

"EXCUSE ME!" I shouted and used my cane to help me stand.

"No need to get upset honey. I'm just hypothetically speaking." She smirked.

"Hypothetically speaking, my husband would never purposely dip out and allow another woman to bear his child. I'd have to be dead and gone before he laid with anyone else. Especially, after the last mistake he made." I was confident in my statement.

"It's a shame my sons gonna lose a good woman." She stood and stretched her arms out.

"But hey. It was nice knowing you."

"If you have something to say Cherisse, just say it. All this beating around the bush shit is stupid."

*DING! DONG!* I turned my head at the sound.

"Bitch are you crazy?" I yelled because she pushed me on the couch to run to the door.

"Hello, we're looking for Cazi Perry." I heard a man's voice and struggled to get up. When she pushed me, I fell on the couch and rolled on the floor.

"He's not here." Cherisse answered.

"Do you know when he'll be here?" I walked to the door and moved his mother out the way.

"I'm his wife Mrs. Perry. Is everything ok?" The cop had a weird look on his face. I'm shocked an officer was here at all because whenever something went down Mark usually showed up.

"Well..." He looked behind, and slid over a little. A woman walked up to the door.

"Hi. I'm from social services and we're looking for Mr. Perry." She extended her hand for me to shake.

"And like I told the officer, I'm his wife. What do you need him for?" Another woman got out the car and went to the back seat.

"Unfortunately, Simone Peterson was murdered a few weeks ago. We've been searching everywhere for your husband."

"Who is Simone Peterson and what does her murder have to do with him? He didn't kill her." Hell yea, I'm standing by my husband. She chuckled a little.

"Here's my husband now." I pointed to him pulling in the driveway.

"Oh, here come the fireworks." Cherisse smiled and leaned on the wall next to where we stood.

"Mrs. Perry, with Ms. Peterson being killed, we had to drop the baby off to the nearest kin."

"Wait, I'm lost."

"Amara?" I heard Cazi calling my name in the background. The cop and lady were directly in front of me which took him outta my view.

"Are you stupid bitch? Cazi had a baby. They're dropping his fucking daughter off." I turned to his mother and back to the two individuals at my door. Did she just say what I think she said?

"So much for being the only woman to bear his kids."

TO BE CONTINUED….